Golden Streak Series Book 4

By

KATHI S. BARTON

World Castle Publishing, LLC

WCP

World Castle Publishing, LLC
Pensacola, Florida

Copyright © Kathi S. Barton 2014
Print ISBN: 9781629890807
eBook ISBN: 9781629890814
First Edition World Castle Publishing, LLC, April 06, 2014
http://www.worldcastlepublishing.com

Cover: Karen Fuller
Editor: Eric Johnston

Chapter 1

Brock opened his eyes, and the first thing he saw was a tattooed ankle. He knew he wasn't in his own bed, much less his own home, but he couldn't for the life of him remember whose home or bed he was in; or for that matter, who the woman was next to him. He rolled to his back and felt a woman behind him well.

"Fuck." He looked up and saw the mirror over the bed just as the woman rolled over. He still had no idea where he was, but the woman's feet told him two things. First, she didn't care about herself overly much, as the polish on her toes was chipped and peeling; and second, they weren't going to be happy with him if either of them woke before he got out of there. After sliding to the end of the bed, he was standing there pulling on his pants when the woman at his back spoke softly.

"You could stay and fuck me again. Millie won't even know if you're quiet." She let the sheet drop to her waist and lifted her breasts up for him. "I'm game if you are."

Millie and Margaret Caldwell were the names; he'd seen their pictures and names in the paper a few times for prostitution and other unsavory things. He shook his head and told her that he had to go. "No thanks. I've got to…I'm sorry, but I must have been really out of it last night to have…how did I get here?"

"Millie decided to dope you up, and we took you here. You're a really big man…well your cock is, but I couldn't tell how tall you were until now. But you didn't wanna have sex with us." She pouted at him. "But we had some fun with each other. Millie and I did it like we always do while you slept away. But now that you're awake and you're not all doped up, we could have some fun. Right?" Brock stared at her for several seconds as she sat there.

"You kidnapped me and brought me here to have sex with me?" She nodded, and he had to sit down. "Did you have a plan, or was just sex all you had in mind?"

"Well, we did hope you'd get one of us knocked up after tonight. Having some of that money you seem to have bunches of would have been really great." She stood up and ran her hands down her body as she moved toward him. "You can still get me pregnant; if you don't, we'll just find someone else, but I'd really like for it to be you. We seen that truck you drive—it's really expensive."

"I bet you would. But I'm afraid that I can't help you with the baby part. You're not my mate, and until I find her, I can't get anyone pregnant." He stood up. "You should have planned this better before trying to get someone like me to have a kid with. What if I would have hurt you or raped you?"

She told him she liked pain a whole lot.

He pulled off his pants and tried to ignore her as she moaned. He didn't even want to think about what she might be doing right now. He folded them neatly and put them on the chair next to his shirt. Taking his shirt and laying it on the floor, he put his boots, pants, and other things in the middle. Then, after making sure he had his wallet and cell phone, he tied it all up in the shirt and tied it loosely around his waist.

He looked at both women now as Millie had woken up. She was looking at him as if she'd never seen a naked man before. But he had a feeling that the two sisters had tried this before, and no telling how many times they'd succeeded…or how many diseases they carried on or in them. He shuddered to think about what a human might have gotten from them.

"I'm going to have to leave here." They looked at the shirt tied around his waist and then up at him. "You're going to have to trust me on this one when I say you're not going to want to fuck with me again — or anyone else for that matter — or else."

"You think we're going to just walk away from this? I got news for you…we're experts at this shit, and you're just going to be another notch on our bank account." Millie stood up and walked to the other side of the bed. "You hit my sister and raped her. It was all I could do just to pull you off her after you comed in her. You're an animal."

Her fist was out before either he or Margaret could react. When Margaret hit the floor and blood erupted from her nose, Millie kicked her several times in the ribs before turning back to him. She was enjoying this…both of them were apparently. The harder her sister kicked her, the louder Margaret's moans became. He had to get the hell out of there.

He smiled at her and let his cat take him. They were about to find out just how right they'd been in calling him an animal. He felt magnificent as a cat, stronger and meaner, too.

Brock snarled at them as they both moved back from him. He wanted to scare them a little more and waved his paw at both of them with his claws extended. When they started to scream, he looked to the window and moved toward it. Shifting to himself, he opened the window and turned to them.

"Fuck with me again and I'll come back here and have you both for dinner. And if I ever hear of you doing this again, or even hear of someone doing this to someone, I will come back here and kill you both. Do you understand?" When they didn't answer, he made a lunging sort of move, and they screamed again. But they both agreed that their doping days were over.

Looking out the window, he realized that he was in a very bad part of town and nearly didn't shift to leap out the window. In the end he jumped and moved quickly to another building before anyone saw him. Being naked in this part of town could get you more than killed; a person could end up with body parts all over the city. While he was in the building next to where he'd been taken, he was pulling on his clothes when he heard the first sirens.

Laughing to himself, he made his way out to the main street and walked toward town, where he hoped his car was. He was nearly there when he heard his phone ring. He answered it with a grin, knowing that whatever his brother Ryland was up to wasn't going to compare to his night.

"You need to go over to the project house on Tenth. Mom is there with some of the contractors, and they said there's a problem. I'm on my way to a board meeting and can't leave unless it's a really huge problem. I'm hoping it is and you call me to come to you." Brock picked up his pace and was just getting to his car at the Lazy Stein when he thought of everything that could be going wrong at a construction site.

"Any idea what's going on so I'm not going there blind?" He was snapping his seatbelt into place after putting his cellphone on his headset when he started the engine. "You know how much I hate walking into something that I don't know. And if Mom is there, I can only assume she was on one of her missions to see to it that everyone was on time to work. You know how much I love this, right?"

"Yes, I do, and nothing about what is going on. Mom was a lot upset, if that tells you anything. But other than that, I have no idea." He paused, and Brock waited. "You're coming over for dinner tonight, right? Jules is coming home from his show, and we're on for his homecoming dinner."

"I'll be there." He had a few things to discuss with his brother as well, like when the hell had he put in that security system, and why didn't he tell him. He'd nearly gotten arrested when he'd gone by to check Jules's house the day before yesterday. It had taken a call to Alistair as well as his mom to get them to back the fuck off and stop waving their guns around.

"Good. I'm going into this meeting now, but call if you need me. Please?" Brock told him he'd do his best and hung up. He pulled into the lot a few minutes later. There were three trucks and an assortment of other cars, including his mom's limo and her driver. Brock tipped his hat at him as he walked by. He could ride in a limo if he wanted, but he preferred to drive himself. He went inside and up to the second floor.

The scene looked like something out of a nightmare. Not that he watched all that much television, but it was still a mess. He had his mom go out of the room where all the blood was and asked one of the workers to stay with her. They knew that it wasn't human blood, but still it had shaken her up a bit. Someone was using the room to send a message to the Goldens. He pulled out his phone and called his brother.

"You don't have to come down here, but I think you should know now because the police have to be called in. Someone has threatened us again, and this time they've done it with blood...pig blood if my nose is correct." Ryland asked what it said. "Basically what it says, or actually what it says?"

"Christ, is it that bad? It's not satanic is it?" Brock told him it wasn't. "Actually what it says. And don't let the police in until I can get there. If we have to be threatened, we might as well show them that we're a family, and not afraid of some small-minded person who has to use blood to make a statement." Brock agreed and read him what was on the wall.

"This blood represents the blood of all you've spilled in the name of progress. The next time we do this it will be the blood of one of you, and it won't be to trash your buildings but to show you we mean business. You'll stop your persecution of the underdog now."

Brock laughed. "What sort of persecution are we making against the underdog again? You're not still trying to hire little kids to polish the silver, are you?"

"Damn, and I thought I was being so careful." Ryland laughed, then sobered. "You've called the cops, but don't say anything until I get there. I'll work on my speech to them on the way over. I'll sound completely confused, which I am, and sorry that we have to deal with this, which again I am. Do you have a clue what might have done this?"

Brock bent down, and using one of his pens, pushed around some papers until he found a pop can. "No, but I think we might get one. They might have left us something to find them with. I'll get it to a friend of mine tonight and see what we can find. Might be one of the workers here that missed the trash can and was too lazy to bend over and pick it up, but you never know."

Ryland said he'd be there soon, and Brock did a little more looking around before the police arrived. They only managed to make the scene worse by walking around like they had their heads up their asses. He found another empty can, as well as some empty blood bags. They'd gotten their "paint" from the local vet if the label on the bags were any indication. It was time to make some calls.

~~~

"I hired someone." Rayne looked up from the planter when her mom spoke. "She's going to be working at the Pretty Flower Two. It's closer for her. And she doesn't drive. I'm not sure why she doesn't, but she doesn't. I would bet it has to do with her childhood, but I can't be sure."

Rayne waited. Her mom was babbling and that wasn't a good sign. She had hired a few people since she and Peter started running Two, and she wondered why she felt the need to tell her about this one. When her mom sat down, then stood again, Rayne wasn't sure she was going to like whatever it was and nearly told her mom just to spill it.

"Her name is Emma Cole, but she goes by Em. She has a great personality once you get to know her. But that's hard if you don't take the time to do it. She's really shy. More shy than any other person I've ever met." Rayne watched her mom pace some more before she continued. "Do you think all people are just mean, or just most of them?"

"What happened to Em, Mom? Did someone hurt her before or after she started working for us?" Her mom sat again and wiped at the tears on her cheeks. "Mom?"

"Both, I think. Actually, I know that she's been hurt before by the scarring she has, but something happened yesterday, too. She's a very lovely girl, but she's...I thought I could keep an eye on her, but I just can't. And Peter tries, but I think she knows what he is, and she's a little afraid of him. He keeps his distance because of what someone has done to her, but—"

"Mom? You're scaring the shit out of me. What happened to her, and why do you feel the need to keep an eye on her?" She stood up to pace again, and Rayne nearly told her to sit. But she was her mom, and she knew better.

"She's a deaf mute. I don't know how it happened, but I would assume she was very young. Someone...something tore at her throat and left a large scar there. As for her deafness, I don't know what caused that. I'm not even sure that she can't talk because of the scar, but she can't. Talk I mean. I'm not even sure that whatever hurt her to leave that scar made it so she couldn't talk either. But when Peter comes around her, she...she nearly cringes."

Rayne thought about how that would hurt her friend Peter. She was on the verge of telling her mom to get rid of the girl but waited to get more information. Something else was going on. "Why is it do you think people are so mean? What did someone do to her that would have you say such a thing? You're normally better around the public than I am."

"One of the customers tried to get her attention by...by screaming at her. When Em didn't turn quickly enough for this person, he grabbed her by the arm and jerked her around. When he did, she...she hit him. I tried to soothe it over, but he wasn't having any of it, and finally I had to call Alistair so he could talk to him. He's coming down today to speak to Em."

She and Neal had been working a show on the waterfront yesterday and hadn't had time to answer their phones even if they would have had service. They'd known that they were going to have spotty service going in and had asked if Alistair and Ryland could help out if there were any problems. Neither man had mentioned it when they'd talked to Neal last night.

"What time is he supposed to meet her? I've got a lot of work to catch up on, and a lot more...." Her mom looked at the doorway, and Rayne closed her eyes. "He's here now."

Her mom nodded. "He wanted to talk to you first. He knows about Em being deaf. She can use sign language, but I'm not sure if he can read it or not. I forgot to ask him when I talked to him. I was really upset at that man, the one that hurt her. She was so upset that I had to have someone take her home. I just hope she doesn't quit. She works really hard."

Rayne got up and went to the sink. She was washing up when her mom spoke again. When she turned, her mom looked like she was on the verge of crying again.

"You can't fire her, honey. I don't think she has any place else to go. And even Peter doesn't want you to do that. We both really like her." She stood up and hugged her. "She's a good, hard worker, but this one man...she carries a notepad around and uses it to talk to other people. I've never had any other issues but with that ugly man who thinks she should be locked away." Rayne wondered what the man would do if Neal shifted in front of him or she zapped him. Probably piss himself.

"Let me talk to Alistair. After that, we'll move on from there. But don't worry about the prick. If he gives me too much trouble, I'll have one of the men eat him for dinner. It might be better than what I want to do to him. And do me a favor, please have her come here for today. I want to get to know her and see if we can work something out with her. Can you have...well not Peter, I guess, but someone bring her here?"

"Yes, I can have Jeff bring her. I think he's sort of sweet on her anyway." Rayne nodded, and her mom left. Alistair came in just as she was pulling out three more orders to fill. She was so glad that she had Ally around to keep her straight and busy. The woman was a miracle in organizing her.

"You have to make sure your employees don't go around knocking the shit out of customers. It could be bad for your business." She glared at him, and he laughed. "Is the girl all right? I hadn't heard that she'd been injured, just that some asshole had jerked her around when she didn't do what he wanted."

"Mom didn't say, so I'm not sure. Jeff is going to bring her over here so that you can talk to her after we talk. You want what I have now, or do you want to wait? Mom gave me some." He nodded and sat at her desk. "The girl's name is Em Cole, and she's a deaf mute. I'm not sure if that's the PC way of saying it, but I'm not in the mood right now to pretty things up. Want to tell me why you didn't tell me yesterday?"

"You sounded tired, and I figured your mom would give you the information. Besides, what could you have done last night at ten o'clock?" She huffed at him, and he smiled. "Neal said your sales were through the roof. How was it really? Is the Pretty Flower going to be the next big thing in floral arrangements?" She flushed and ignored his question about the next big thing. She'd be happy if she was the next little thing.

"We never stopped. I'm so glad he talked me into taking that extra inventory or we would have been standing around with our thumbs up our ass at around noon. Saul brought us lunch, and we had him go back and grab up anything else that wasn't nailed down from all three shops, and still only came home with empty containers. We sold it all." She smiled when she thought of the success of their first outdoor show. "I think we might be able to hang on for another year if this keeps up."

She still couldn't believe she had two shops and a warehouse. Every time one of the huge greenhouses she dealt with had extra inventory or a back haul, she and her crew scrambled to make room for whatever inventory they had. And just the day before yesterday, one of them had approached her and Neal about taking their end of year things for next to nothing. They were going to be overflowing with merchandise in a few days.

She sat down. "The man grabbed her because she couldn't hear him. Mom said she carries around a pad of paper to communicate, and she's never had any issues before this. Why would someone grab another person they don't know?"

"I took a call from him this morning before I left the office. That man is a shit. He said he thought you shouldn't have people like her working if she couldn't do her job. He said that she'd embarrassed him by not listening to him. I explained to him that she was handicapped, but that just set him off more." He handed her some notes. "He wants to sue you and your company. But I have a plan."

"Of course you do. How much is this going to cost me? Or do you think we can just kidnap him and bring him somewhere remote so you all can have a nice snack? I'll provide the beer." He laughed and acted like she'd wounded him. "Seriously, I can't fire her, and I wouldn't even if that were part of the plan. She doesn't deserve what he did to her."

"You're right. You don't want to fire her. But I really do have a plan. I have this friend who is going to run an article on your hiring people to work that are having a rough time. She's going to point out that you have several handicapped people working…why are you shaking your head? I've already spoken to several of your staff, and they are all for it. They seem to think you're this goddess that others need to know about."

"You did not speak to any of them." He nodded. "Damn it, Alistair, I do this because they need a helping hand, not to get more sales."

"I know that, and they do as well. Jeff? You said he's coming here. How much did it cost you to renovate the van so he could drive it for you?" She flushed. "And that woman Debra, the one that is paralyzed from the waist down. When you hired her, you also bought her a wheelchair that she could move around in. What do you suppose other places would have done?"

"I'm not other places." He laughed at her. "I'm not saying I agree with it or even if I want you to run it, but what is this article going to prove? What's it supposed to do other than make me out to be some sort of idiot?"

"No one thinks you're an idiot, love. And this article is to show others what we all already know. You're a kind and loving woman who will do this for me so that I can tell my wife that you're going to stay in business. She's afraid if you close up she won't have a job anymore."

Rayne snorted. "She won't let me pay her, so technically she doesn't have a job working for me. And whatever I should be paying her, she and your family spends twice that on flowers. I can't imagine where on earth they're putting them all. Every time I get something new in, they all rush here to be the first to get it. They've even taken to showing up on truck days to see what comes off it." She got up to pace, embarrassed and pleased that they liked her shop so much. "This article is going to bring in every crackpot in the whole town to see the freak show they think I have working here. That might be good for what's going on now, but I don't need a fucking circus around here when I'm trying to work."

"Some will come out to see, yes, but not most of them. You might even get an influx of applicants, too, but that wouldn't be so bad, would it? I know you're planning to expand next summer, so that could help you as well." She nodded at him. "Not to mention that if you and Neal ever take a honeymoon, you won't have to worry about the shops so much if you have enough people working here."

A woman knocked on the door jamb, and both she and Alistair stood up. Christ, her mom wasn't kidding about her being lovely. She looked like what Rayne had thought an Emma would look like. She was blonde with blue eyes, delicate and soft looking. She moved into the room without taking Alistair's hand, pulled out her notepad, and handed her the top sheet. Rayne looked at it, then at the girl, and handed it back to her.

"No, I won't accept your resignation. And I have no intentions of firing you." She started to write again, and

Rayne touched her arm. The connection was immediate. *"You can speak to me this way if you'd like and I'll tell him. His name is Alistair Golden, and he's my attorney, so you can say whatever you want to say around him and it won't go any further. But you won't quit working for me. That bastard wins if you do, and I so don't want that to happen."*

"He will take everything from you. Men like him only do things like this because they are cheaters and liars. That man will leave you alone if he doesn't see me anymore. I won't let that happen just because I'm deformed." She looked at Alistair. *"He will agree with you despite the fact that he's an attorney. Ask him."*

"She thinks that if she quits that everything will just go away. She wants me to accept her resignation so that the man who grabbed her will give up." Alistair was shaking his head before she finished. For now Rayne was going to ignore the deformed remark and have a talk with her later about it. "Em and I can speak using a link. You ask her and I'll relay the questions and what she says. But I won't allow her to quit."

"Neither will I." She told Em what he had said. "Ask her if I may ask her a few questions about yesterday. Tell her that I need as much information as she can remember, as well as what she thought the man said to her. Did he hurt her? And if so, does she need medical attention? I would also like to talk to her about the article and see if she would mind being interviewed."

She relayed the questions to Em and told her about the newspaper article. Em stared at Alistair, then at her before answering. She could already see that she wasn't going to do it. She could almost feel the girl's fear.

"I can't help you with that. If you make me, I'll have to leave here." Em looked around the room, and Rayne would bet that she took everything in and knew where everything

was, including the windows and exits. *"I can't let anyone from my family find me. They would drag me home again to be their servant. I'm not going back."* There was a great deal of hatred in her voice, and she wasn't surprised to feel her fear double. Whoever her family was, they hadn't left a warm and fuzzy feeling in their daughter. Rayne would bet that her handicap as well as the scarring had something to do with them. But she'd never pry beyond talking to her unless it became an issue later.

"As long as you work for me no one will force you into doing anything you don't want to. And if anyone tries, you come to me. We protect those that work for us." The woman nodded, but Rayne had a feeling that she didn't believe her. She didn't blame her; she wasn't one to trust quickly either.

Em and Alistair sat at her work table, and Rayne sat at her workstation. She could fill pots while helping Alistair relay questions and answers. A couple of times she wanted to find the man who had hurt Em and knock the shit out of him, but she knew that she'd just make it harder on Alistair and Neal if they had to bail her out of jail.

Alistair took pictures of the bruising on her arm as well as the scratches she had. Her hand was also bruised, and he took pictures of that as well. Before he left, Alistair told her that he wanted to find the slimy bastard and hurt him a few times. She offered to bring the beer again, and he told her he'd let her know. The man was going to find himself in a world of hurt now, she figured.

Chapter 2

Brock read the article in the paper three times and laughed harder each time. The women he'd been kidnapped by had actually told the police that a giant tiger had tried to rape them. He laughed out loud when he got to the part where the person who had written the article had put his own slant on the story. He thought that the women were known to be drug addicts and that most of their police records were for robbery and solicitation. He had gone on to say that while he had covered the story, there were no other sightings of a tiger in the area, and none had escaped from any zoos or wildlife preserves within the five-state area. He had made it sound as if he hadn't really expected to, either.

"Did you see this?" Ryland tossed the same paper on his desk in front of him as soon as he entered his office. "I don't suppose if I were to check with any of the rest of the family they'd know anything about it either."

"It was me." His brother sat down and glared. "Don't get your underpants in a twist, Ryland. Even though I was the tiger, I wasn't the bad guy. What the article doesn't tell you and I will is that they drugged me with a date rape drug and took me to their lair—for lack of a better term—and decided to have sex with me, hoping I would get one of them pregnant. And before you ask, no, they didn't know who I was. They said I have a nice truck that looked expensive."

"But you shifted in front of them." He nodded. "What the fuck for? What if they'd had a camera or, Christ, if they were videotaping the whole thing?"

"I would have heard it and, to be honest with you, I think together they couldn't think their way out of a paper bag even if it were wet. Not to mention since they were both naked, it would have been really hard for me not to see a camera they might have had pointed at me. Their names are Millie and Margaret Caldwell. I believe if you think about it, their names will ring a bell. If not, then do a search on them. You'll be amazed at what the two of them have tried since they learned to swindle people. I think they've both been to jail more times than I've been wasted."

His brother leaned back in the chair. "I don't like this, but the article makes them sound like a couple of crack heads, so I'm willing to let it go. But this thing with the building downtown, what have you been able to find out? Other than, of course, that the blood was pigs."

"The prints on the cans matched the DNA on the rim, so I've run them and figured out who they are. They have a record for vandalism but little else, other than the father has a great deal of drunken and disorderly. I'm running some things now, and I think maybe the father worked for us a few years back and caused us some problems until we had to get rid of him before someone got hurt. He might be our scumbag in this case, or so they think. But I want to look deeper before I give you that. It sounds to me like a case of kids thinking they might be helping out poor old dad." Ryland asked their names. "Owens, Harvey Owens that worked for the construction company that we bought up and sold out in chunks. Harvey has two sons, Harvey Jr. and Donny. The older goes by Junior. He and Donny are nineteen and seventeen respectively, but the older has been a great deal of trouble since their dad was fired. Mostly more of the shit they did to us, but with overpasses and trains. Junior is going to be facing some hard times if he's arrested again. Donny, I don't know. I think he might be bullied into what happened. I've talked to his teacher at the high school. She's been trying her best to get him to apply for good colleges, but the father and older brother aren't helping her."

"So he's smart and the other members of his family aren't. I can see where the kid might be having problems, but they did trash our building. What's the plan with them?" Brock tossed him a file and waited while he looked it over. "You have pictures of them doing this?"

"Video, too, but it's just more of what you see there in front of you. I had set up the camera system about a month ago because I'd gotten a good deal on it and wanted to try it out there. It was an empty building not set for any sort of reconstruction for a while, and after finding out the system worked, I left it there so I'd know where it was if and when I needed it. I guess I sort of forgot about it until one of the cops asked if we might have the place on any type of alarm system." He handed him another file. "I think we could benefit from purchasing more like it and putting them in the other buildings we have that are empty. Maybe just the entrance and exits, but it would pay for itself if anything like this happened again."

Ryland handed him back both folders. "Do it. And press charges against the older boy, but not the younger. We don't see him in these. Maybe we'll find out he has some redeeming qualities and we can get him to work by cleaning up his mess. Let me know what you figure out with their dad. Maybe the apple doesn't fall all that far from the tree."

Brock asked him about the thing with Rayne. "I heard that Alistair had to go down and straighten out a few things with one of her customers. And there was a girl involved that got hurt. Anything you want me to get involved in?"

"I don't know, but I'd ask Alistair. The girl's name is Em Cole, and she works at Two but seems to be fine. The man was going to press charges last I heard because the girl hit him between the eyes when he grabbed her. I think Alistair is working on an angle to get that to go away. Apparently this guy is a known hothead, and has done stupid shit like this before."

Brock asked him if he thought that the plant shops could use some of the cameras as well. He laughed when Ryland glared at him. He and Rayne had been going around and around since she'd become a member of the family, and Brock loved to poke the bear, either one of them, every chance he got.

He placed an order for the cameras and made a few more calls to find out what he could on Harvey Owens. It was noon when he realized that he'd skipped breakfast and was now starving. He decided to make a trip out to see Rayne and see if he could convince her to get some cameras too. He might even tell her that Ryland thought it was a dumb idea just to get her to do it.

A truck was pulling in as he got there. He wondered if it was one of the ones she'd made a deal on and was happy for her and Neal. They were going to make this work, and he'd never been prouder of them both. As he pulled up on the other side of the large semi, he got out when the driver did.

"This place ain't as easy to find as I was told. 'Course there was a shit ton of traffic too." Brock took an immediate and profound dislike for the guy and felt his cat stir along his skin. "You might want to tell the little woman that when she says to get off the exit, she should say that it's a mile and a quarter, not a little over a mile."

"A mile and a quarter is a little over a mile." He asked the man for paperwork, and after telling Brock he didn't have any, the man asked Brock if he was there to help unload. "No. And you're not unloading without paperwork." The man took a stance that his cat and his beast didn't care for. Both of them snarled at him to be released.

"Now see here. I got me a load to get rid of, and she will by God take it." Brock stood very still and waited on the man to make another move with the ball bat that suddenly appeared in his hand. He felt Neal coming toward him and turned just as he reached him.

"He claims he has a load, yet he doesn't have any paperwork. When I asked him for it, he got a tad pissy with me." Neal looked at the driver, then back at Brock. "Do we take it?"

"Not without paperwork, we don't." The man advanced toward them just as Rayne came out of the back end of the shop. She was not looking all that happy either.

"You might want to turn this rig around because whatever you're hauling, I'm not taking." The driver looked at her and then at them. "And looking to them isn't going to get you any help either. I run the show here, and if you have any doubts about that, I'll use that bat for more than just pounding your head in. I'll make sure I shove it where the sun doesn't shine."

"You're supposed to take all the loads that are dropped here. I'm dropping this load if I have to leave the trailer and come back for it later. I'm not backhauling when someone from your outfit said they'd take it off my hands." Rayne walked within a few inches of the man, and he took a step back. Brock saw her cat shimmer along her skin, and he was sure that the man had as well.

Instead of saying anything to the man, she pulled out her cell phone and watched him. Brock would not fuck with Rayne on a good day, and this didn't look to him like it was one. When she turned her back on the driver, he reached for her the exact moment that Rayne put her hand out. When he touched her, he fell to the ground twitching. Neither he nor Neal went to the man.

"Hello, this is Rayne Golden, and I have…. Yes, that's true. Yes, I'm sure, but…. No. And, hell no." She turned to look at Neal and him. "And what did this man look like that you…? Oh, I see…and when was this again?"

She told the person to wait and went to the back of the trailer and read off the seal numbers on it, then all the other numbers on the back. The trailer number was first, then the license plate. Then she went to the front of the rig and flipped the man over and took out his wallet.

"It says here his name is Doug P. Hamilton and he's from Iowa. And, yes, before you ask me again, he did claim he had no paperwork." There was a long pause, and then she turned to him. "Call the police for me, would you, Brock? And Neal? I would like it if you were to go and get some tie-down rope and tie our man up while we wait."

Brock pulled out his phone and made the call. He could see that Rayne was upset and didn't want to make her more so. As she put her own cell phone away, she helped Neal tie the man up who was just coming around.

"What going on, love?" Neal held her in his arms. "Did he steal this load? Or is it something else?"

"He stole it from the distributor three days ago. It was sitting on a lot attached to another truck, and he took it and killed the man that was driving the rig. They have it on tape at the rest stop. There's a manhunt out for him as we speak." She looked up at him. "He was bringing it here to hide it for a few days. Then if no one caught him, he was going to take it on to somewhere else to sell it off. The woman I spoke to said that there has been a bulletin out on the trailer since it was taken, and she had me verify all the numbers. When the police get here, we're supposed to have them call her back and she'll walk them through opening the seal and seeing if what's supposed to be in it is actually there."

When the police arrived, Jake Rider, Brock's drinking buddy, had him hold the phone while he cut the seal. The trailer was loaded, and he could see even from where he was standing on the ground that it wasn't plants or dirt. He saw the car before he saw anything else.

"It's two cars, and I'd say that one of them is worth more than I make in two or so years." Jake laughed as he continued speaking to the dispatcher. "Yes, ma'am, I'd think that was about right. The man who first found him is Brock Golden. Want I should put this driver up for you until you can get the proper paperwork down here to me? Yes, ma'am, I can do that too. It would be my pleasure, actually, to help out." He looked at Brock.

"Are you busting up car thefts now, Jake, or does that get in the way with your flirting with women over the phone?"

Jake flushed. "She said that the owner of these here cars is giving a reward to the person who finds them. I told her that would be you since you stopped him from dropping and running off until the heat was off. She said that she'd seen this before and was glad that someone had the sense not to take a load without paperwork. She sure was happy to get these back for him. Then there is the little matter of him killing the driver. She said the police in Iowa are gonna be really happy like to have him back. They have a nice little cell just waiting for him."

Brock helped Jake load the man into the cruiser and made sure he hit his head a few times in the process. He could have been gentler, but what fun would there be in that? Besides, he was pretty sure that Jake had a little party waiting for him back at the jail. He was forever getting flowers for his pretty wife, and Rayne gave him a good frequent buyer discount.

~~~

Em watched the lot. As soon as the police had shown up, she'd found herself a hole to hide in and stayed there. She was still waiting for the police to leave when a shadow fell across her. She turned slightly to see a customer moving by her slowly and speaking to the woman next to her.

She could read lips but didn't much care for it. Most of the time, people would look away from her and she'd only get a portion of what they were saying. The notepad worked best here, and people didn't seem to mind her writing her answers to their questions, but there were a few that didn't have the patience to wait for her and would walk away. If the person had been mean to anyone else in the shop, she'd take a lot longer to write and smiled when they walked away. She looked back at the lot when the customer moved on.

The man she'd met earlier was standing next to another man who looked like he could almost be his twin. But this man was taller than Neal and much broader. He looked as if he worked out a great deal and probably took some sort of drugs to help him look like one of those big weightlifters. But for whatever reason she didn't think so. She would also bet that he didn't work out at one of those fancy gyms like she'd seen on television either, but got his muscles from hard work and sweat.

When the police left with the driver of the big truck, she moved out of her space and back onto the sales floor. She was watering the plants when she realized someone was close to her.

It was Neal. He smiled at her and nodded to the man next to him. Neal used sign language to tell her who he was. "This is my brother Brock. He works with us sometimes, and when he's around, I want you to feel comfortable. I try to introduce all the new hires to all my brothers in the event you see them hanging around."

She took a step back when he took two toward her. She was suddenly afraid of the bigger man and what he might do to her. She whimpered. Neal touched the man's shoulder when he turned to him. She couldn't tell what they were saying because they weren't looking at her any longer, but she knew that whatever it was couldn't bode well for her.

When the man reached for her again, she pulled further away and looked at him. He was smiling, but she wasn't stupid enough to think it meant he was being friendly. She looked at his mouth again when it started moving.

"I won't hurt you, I promise you." She shook her head, and he backed up. "I won't harm you, Em. I can't."

She had no idea what that was supposed to mean. He was twice her size in weight, and he was a good foot taller than her. She looked at Neal, who was waving at his wife. She was desperate to know what was going on, and when Rayne touched her arm, she let her. The men were frightening her.

"This is my brother-in-law Brock. He wants you to know that he won't hurt you, but he would like to touch you for a moment. He has...he thinks you might be something to him." Rayne glared at Brock. *"He's a nice guy most of the time, unless he's scaring my employees. Can he touch your arm? I swear that's all he'd better do."*

Em was nodding before she could think of all the reasons why this was a bad idea. But even as his hands grazed her bare arm, something inside of her melted and she was more afraid than before, but not so much of the man but of what she was feeling. He smiled at her again and pulled her gently to him. She went because she felt she had no choice. Her heart was telling her it was fine, while her mind was telling her to back the fuck up.

When he buried his face in her neck, she felt him...she thought he purred. When he licked her skin, her body seemed to catch fire, and she backed away from him, or at least she tried to. Something was off about this whole thing, and she wanted away from him.

"You're his mate. Do you know what that means?" She shook her head at Rayne, not because she didn't know what it meant—because she did—but she didn't want him near her. *"Em, listen to me, I won't let him hurt you. He's a good man, and he just wants to talk to you."*

"He's not human, is he? He's like that other man, Peter. Is he?" Rayne shook her head, but before she could answer her, Em nodded. *"He is. That man who tried to bite me said I was his mate, too, and that he wanted me as his bride. I would rather die than let anyone bite me again."*

Rayne spoke to the two men and the one that had licked her, Brock, looked at her throat, and she felt like he'd burned her. Not a bad feeling, but...she looked at him when Rayne turned back to her.

"He wants to know when this happened and if the vampire is still alive?" She nodded her head. *"Brock isn't a vampire, Em, he's a tiger like me. My mom is a wolf, but I'm a tiger."*

"How is that possible? You can't be a tiger, you're...you're human like me. That man that bit me, he was...oh my God, what have I done?"

Em looked around, frantic for a place to run, but they were closing in on her, and she felt herself grow faint. She was just reaching for something to protect herself with or at least somewhere to hide from them all when Rayne touched her. She felt a slight pinch-like feeling in her head, then things went blurry. As she tumbled forward, she saw Brock reach for her, and thought that if she had to be caught by someone that he would do nicely.

She must have only been out for a few seconds, because when she opened her eyes, he was still carrying her. She struggled a little, but he was bigger, and she could see the hard cords in his neck when she tried to fight him. She was surprised to find that while she was afraid, she wasn't of him. She was being put on the sofa in the lunch room when she realized that they were alone.

"I'm going to sit with you until you get some color back. You're as white as a ghost." She nodded. "Would you like something to drink? I would, but I doubt very much that Rayne has anything stronger than cola or tea."

"Water," she told him and waited to see if he could understand. When it was apparent that he couldn't read

sign language, she wrote it on her pad and handed it to him. He went to the refrigerator and handed her a bottle of water.

"You must go through a lot of those when you're trying to have a long conversation." She looked down at the pad and then up at him. "I could get you a deal on them wholesale, or you could teach me how to understand."

"Why?" He sat down next to her as she continued writing. "I work at the other shop and will not see you."

He lifted her chin so she could see his mouth. "I will be where you are. You know what I am to you?"

"I don't care." He nodded. "You will have to find someone else. I won't be a whore to any man."

Brock took her pen and paper and read her note. She knew that he could read it fine in her hand and wanted to snatch it back from him, but he simply tore off the sheet and wadded it up before writing her a note.

"I don't want a whore in my life. I want someone to love and to cherish. You would never be my whore, and I'll kill any man who would think that of you." He signed his name and handed it back to her, slipped off the sofa, and sat in front of her. "I'm not going to let you think horrible things about what is going on between us. I'll come in tomorrow, and we'll get to know each other. Okay?"

She shook her head, and he stood up. She watched him as he went to the door, where he turned and walked back toward her. Em let him take the notepad from her fingers and waited while he wrote on it again. When he kissed her on the nose, she was so startled that she didn't react until he was out of sight. Then she looked down at the note he'd given her.

It was phone numbers, four of them, as a matter of fact, each one of them labeled with a place. Work had two numbers, his home number, as well as his cell phone number. And under those was *"if you need me, call me for anything."*

"Are you all right?" She nodded at the voice in her head and realized that Rayne couldn't see her, and told her she was. *"Good. I would like to have you come out and help Mom on the register for a little while. She has to leave soon to get our lunch, and she thinks you can run the register for her. And if you want, you can ask me any questions you might have about Brock. He gave me permission to tell you what a fabulous person he is."* Em was sure he probably was, but she had no use for him.

"I can't run the register for you. What if someone has a question? What if I mess up and lose all the money?" She was panicky and was pretty sure Rayne knew it. *"You should just let me water the plants and stuff. I'm pretty good at that, and they don't ask me questions."*

"I should hope not. And you can do anything you want if you put your mind to it. Also, if they have a question you can't answer, call me through our link. You can do that, but I have a feeling you can answer anything that needs to be addressed." Em had never had anyone have so much confidence in her before, and wasn't sure what to do about it.

"Brock said that he would be back tomorrow to speak with me. Do you think you could ask him to stay away? I don't want him as my mate or anything else. I don't want anything to do with him." She had a feeling that Rayne wouldn't ask him, but it didn't hurt to ask.

"No. If you want him to stay away, then you tell him. If you know what a mate is, then you have a pretty good idea of how they are when it comes to their mates. And Brock is very protective of his friends. I can only imagine what he'd do to protect you."

"*I don't need a protector. I just want to be left alone.*" Rayne laughed, and Em felt herself grow angry. "*I'm not being funny. I do not want him to come near me. He makes me feel all mushy inside.*"

"*If you tell him that, then you'll never get rid of him. But I'm letting you know right now that it will do you little good to tell him, and you just might find he's not so bad once you get to know him.*"

That was the problem; she didn't want to get to know him, or anyone else for that matter. If it wasn't for the fact that she needed a job, she would have left when she could after the man had grabbed her at the other shop.

Em went to the cash register and watched Karin ring out a few customers. Everything was marked on it, and if there wasn't a price on something, a sheet with prices on it was in a large notebook near her that had pictures of everything that they sold. As soon as she rang out the first customer on her own, Karin left. Em had never been so proud and terrified in her entire life. She hoped Karin returned soon because, for as much as she wanted to crawl away and hide, she wanted to make this work even more.

Chapter 3

Brock was just finishing up for the day when Bronwyn knocked on his open door. She'd been in Ryland's office for the better part of the afternoon and now came down to bother him. He looked at her when she sat the baby carrier down and glared at him.

"Were you going to tell me?" He shrugged. "I have as much right to know what's going on as anyone else. Why did I have to hear about your finding your mate from Neal when he called to tell me that he was going to be late to dinner? And what do you think your mom is going to say?"

"She told me that she was glad for me and to bring her by for dinner soon. I told her, like I will you, that I don't want you to go down there and welcome her to the family because she doesn't trust me as yet, and I need to make her see that I won't harm her. Rayne seems to think she'll bolt if given enough reason to do so."

"Someone hurt her?" He nodded. "Do you know who yet? And when you find out, will you tell me so that I can beat the ever loving shit out of him? I may be a mom, but I'm one shit kicker when I need to be."

"Yes, you can be, but I think I can handle her for now. You don't even know her yet and you're already willing to protect her for me?" She smiled at him. "I'll take care of the man, whoever he was. I have a feeling it's a vampire, just so you know. She's terrified of Peter, and when Rayne told her that we were cats, she didn't seem all that surprised. I think she's aware of us, but that doesn't mean she likes us overly much." At least she'd let him touch her. Now he had to convince her that he wasn't going to hurt her too. That, he figured, was going to be a great deal harder.

"Neal told Ryland that she couldn't hear or speak. Do you know if the vampire did that to her or not?" He told her that he thought so but again didn't know for sure. "What have you found out about her?"

"Not much. She's twenty-five and single. Her father is alive, as is her mother. She's in a mental institution, however, and has been for the past several years. There are four brothers, all of them about as useless as they come, and Em is the middle child. None of the men, as far as I can tell, have held anything more than a fast-food job for more than a month, and that was a very long time ago." He handed her the address that he'd been able to find. "They're living in a house that has the utilities and other things paid monthly by a trust, though I'm still digging into that to figure out by whom. No phone service and no cell either, at least in their names. The father gets a check monthly from a settlement from about the time the mother went to the mental institution, but it's not enough to afford the house that they're living in. I'm still chasing down what the mother is locked away for."

"You've been busy." He handed her the papers that had been on the printer, and she looked the pictures over. "She looks like her mother. And her brothers look like they haven't missed a meal for some time. Do you suppose she's hiding from them?"

"I think so. She left home about eight years ago under odd circumstances. She'd been hospitalized for something, and when she disappeared the day before her release, her father threw a fit and demanded that they produce her. I talked to one of the doctors there, and he said that the man said they were keeping her from them. He wouldn't tell me what she'd been in for other than to say that he hoped she stayed gone for her safety." He took back the pictures and put them in the file with the other things he'd found. "Do you think I'm wrong in doing this sort of search on her?"

She looked at him. "Do you?"

He did in a way, but he also knew from experience that the more you knew the better equipped you were to be able to handle a crisis. And this had the markings for one. He looked at little Gabriella as she stirred in her seat, and walked around to pick her up.

"When she was born, what did you think about? Right after Rayne handed her to you, what was your first thought?" He snuggled the little girl against his neck and smiled when she giggled.

"I thought 'holy mother fuck, I'm a mother.' Then I looked at her and fell completely in love. She's not as hard to take care of as I thought. Of course, I have help, but she's...why?"

"When I touched Em and licked her throat, I felt my life center. I know it sounds really stupid after just one touch, but she made me think I was both king of the world and the lowest part of pond scum as I could be." She laughed and took Gabriella from him when he handed her to her. "She was terrified of me. Not just of what I was to her, but of me. I think that one of those men in that picture is the reason for it, other than the vampire. I think her family is going to piss me off and I'm going to have to put them in their place before this is all over. And I'm thinking that the place will be marked with a nice marble headstone that I can piss on when the mood strikes me."

"Again, I ask you why you think this when you've only seen a few pictures and haven't even bonded with her enough to know anything about her."

He nodded and went back to his desk and handed her the last thing he'd been able to find. She read it and then looked up at him. "Her brother tried to drown her? What the hell did he do that for? And why the hell isn't he in prison?"

It was a newspaper article from about the time that Em had been a year old. Her brother, Wilfred Cole and second oldest of the children, had been watching his sister while the father was absent. The paper hadn't said where he'd been or how long he'd been gone, just that he was absent from the home. The boy, six at the time, had decided to give his sister a bath. When she wouldn't stop screaming, he held her under the water in the hopes of making her go quiet, he'd told the police when they'd arrived on scene.

"He was made to see someone, and I can only assume it was a psychiatrist. I can't find out any information about the sessions other than he went to them and his father didn't. He'd been at the hospital with the little girl for the first one, then after that...." Brock shrugged. "This doctor friend of mine told me that she might have had some damage to her brain and it caused her not to hear or speak. He said while it's not common, the brain is something that no one has a clear grasp on totally."

Rayne stood up. "I'd see what I can find out about where the girl is living if I were you. I did a little digging myself and found that she only gave a post office box for her address. I would hate to find out she's been living like I did, and without near the protection I had for myself."

He'd already been looking into that and told her so. "I'm going to try and see her tonight before she gets off work. If I can, would it be all right with you if I brought her to dinner tonight? I know that it's family only for Jules's homecoming, but she might do well to see us all together."

"As of the moment you found her, she became family. Bring her if you can, but don't force it." She picked up Gabriella and moved to the door, and stopped to look at him. "I'll touch her and see what I can find out for you, but…Brock, I want you to be careful of this. Not of your mate, but the men who we both think are trying to find her. I have a feeling that they aren't nearly as stupid as we think."

"I will." He'd nearly told her he could handle anything they put to him, but he could see that she was worried. He stood up and walked her to the elevator, and when she was gone, he looked at May, his secretary. "Do you think you can find something for me from one of your many sources?"

"Of course I can. What do you need to know?" He grinned. "I don't think I like that look. It sort of says to me that you're going to want more than just a few tidbits I can find by calling in some smallish favors."

"I need you to find out why a woman by the name of Robin Cole is in a mental institution and how long she's been there." She shook her head at him. "You won't?"

"I know who she is. If you ever read the paper instead of just the sports section, you would, too. She tried to murder her children. She claimed that they were all vampires and that they were going to suck her dry." She clicked a few keys on her computer. "She went by her maiden name at the time, as she said she wasn't really married to the man who had fathered her children, and she wanted nothing to do with him. The only reason I know her name is because a friend of mine was in the courthouse when she was brought in for trial. She said that Gilbert Cole and her sons were all made into vampires, and she wanted to stake them. Of course, she was put away for a while, but not in a mental institution. That's where she ended up a few months ago when she tried to slit her wrists and nearly succeeded. Here it is."

He read over her shoulder how the woman had claimed that her sons and the man that she'd been wed to were now the living dead. She claimed that if no one did anything, she was going to. At the time, her children's ages ranged from twenty-two to thirteen, and she claimed that even her supposed husband was a vampire. She was adamant that her daughter was innocent, but if no one would save her, then she, too, would be as dead as them. Em would have been seventeen when it happened.

"She *was* nuts." Brock couldn't agree more. "But see, she's been out of it for a few months now. I think she was put away about the time your niece was born. Anyway, they said she'd been cleared of all the charges, but the attempt of suicide was a cry for help, and they put her away where she would be able to get treatments. It had been a postpartum problem. That's what they claimed at the beginning, and that has since been taken care of with drugs."

He sat on her desk and tried to think about what this might mean for Em, or even if she knew. He went to his office and gathered up his things, and tried to think of a plausible reason for stopping by the flower shop to see her when he looked at May's desk. Of course, he needed a flower for his office. And he knew just the person who could help him.

~~~

Em was ringing out a customer when Brock walked in. She'd managed to only think of him about a hundred times today, and now here he was. She tried her best to ignore him, but when he sat on the counter and grinned at her, she wanted to hide in the office.

"I've been thinking about you today." She didn't know what to say to him, so she started wiping the dirt off the counter. When he touched her arm, she looked at him. "You'll have to keep looking at me, love, if we're going to get to know each other."

She took out her pad and wrote him a note. "I don't want to get to know you. I like not knowing you at all. Go away."

"Nope," he told her with that grin again that made her feel all tingly and mushy again. "I wanted to invite you to have dinner at my mom's house. My brother Jules has been gone a month, and we're having a party for him." She shook her head. "Okay, then I'll hang out at your house, and we'll watch television."

"I don't have a TV, and I don't want you to hang out with me. Don't you have someone else that you can bother?"

He jumped off the counter and stood behind her as she rang up a customer. When she realized he was speaking with the man, she grew even more nervous about him being so close. When the man turned to her, she wondered if Brock had told him that she was deformed and what else he'd said. But the man only handed her cash and smiled at her. She gave him back his change and watched him leave.

"What did you tell him? He's mean whenever he comes into the shop across town, and won't speak to anyone."

He took the note and sat down again. "I told him that you were learning a new trade today and would he mind smiling at you because you were so nervous. He said you always have a smile for him when he comes in down at the other shop, and he loved seeing you here. He goes across town to see you smile for him." She looked at him to see if he was kidding and couldn't tell. The man was driving her insane.

When he stared at her for so long, she wondered if she had food on her mouth. She licked her lips to be sure. She didn't understand men, and this one was proving to be the hardest of all. When he stood up and ran his finger down her throat, she felt his touch like he'd set a match to her. She lifted her head to look at him.

"Do it again." She didn't know what he meant, but the harder he looked at her mouth, the more she felt the need to lick her lips again. When she did, he lowered his head to her, and she knew that he was going to kiss her. And for as much as she wanted him to do it, she wanted to tell him to back off. But when his mouth brushed gently over hers, she had to grab onto his arms to steady her.

The second time his mouth touched hers, it was firmer, and he suckled her lower lip into his mouth and nibbled on it. She swayed forward, and he wrapped his arm around her and pulled her to his body as he deepened the kiss. The moment they were flush against one another, she felt her world tilt more until he was the only support she needed. As he lifted his head, she felt her entire body cry out.

"You're so beautiful." He kissed her again, and she felt something like hunger come from him. "I would like nothing more than to lay you out on this counter and make love to you, but I won't be able to stop until you're mine."

She didn't want him to let her go, but she knew that him holding her was going to be trouble. She might not have a lot of experience with sex, but she knew when a man wanted her. And his erection felt as big as her arm.

When he let her go, she stepped back but grabbed the counter behind her. She didn't know what to do now. When he moved to the other side of the counter, she went to the cash register and waited for the woman who was making her way toward her. She didn't have much, but she was something to take her mind off the man sitting so near, yet who felt as if he were miles away.

Writing in her pad, she asked the woman if she'd found everything she needed. The woman read the note and handed it back to her with a frown. When she looked at Brock, so did she. He took the note and then read it to her.

Her hands started to fly as she spoke to her. Her name was Cassandra White, and she was a teacher at the local deaf school. She also asked if the shop had any African violets that were already potted.

"Yes," Em told her. "I know that the boss was working on some this morning, and I'll see if she's finished with them yet."

As she walked toward where she knew Rayne was, she reached for her boss and told her about the order and what she'd told the woman. Rayne laughed and told her to give her two minutes, and she'd have one finished for her. She also told her that she was proud of her for thinking on her feet so quickly. When she entered the workstation, she saw that Rayne and the vampire were back there, and she turned to go.

"Wait. He would like to speak to you. Peter feels badly that you dislike him so much. He wants to know if he's done something wrong or has hurt you in any way."

She shook her head. "I don't dislike him. I just...he is a vampire, and I...I want nothing to do with them and their kind. He is...I don't want anything to do with him."

"Then I'm sorry, Em, but if you want to work here, you're going to have to give me a better reason than that to treat one of my dearest friends this way. He's willing to meet you halfway, but you're not even trying."

She looked at Rayne as she handed her the little violet. It was a bright purple, but mostly it was blurry. She was being fired. Nodding once, she moved toward the cash register and blindly rung the rest of the things the teacher had up. Then she went to the back room to get her things.

Em wasn't sure how she was going to get home from here, but she'd walk it if she had to. When she started back out of the break room, the vampire was standing there. He asked her if she had just a moment.

"I need to go, please. I no longer work here, and I would just like to go home." He nodded but stepped in front of her when she tried to go around him. "I want to leave."

"I can't let you go like this. I need to...I would please like to know who bit you." She looked at him, terrified. "I can tell if you would just let me touch the wound. I won't harm you in any way."

She put her hand over her throat and stepped back. He didn't move, but she thought that if she lowered her hand he'd bite her before she could run. When she backed into someone and they wrapped their arms around her, she felt dizzy with fear and turned on the person, and started to tear at his face and anything else she could get at. Then suddenly she couldn't move.

"Take deep breaths. Stop fighting me, you can't break me. Take a fucking breath before you pass out. Open your eyes too." Her breath came back into her body like she'd had something fill her. She looked at the people standing around her and realized she was lying on the floor. Then she saw Brock.

She'd clawed him. His face looked like she'd torn him so deeply in places that he'd need stitches. When he smiled at her, she could see that his lip was bloodied and that blood was even on his teeth. Em started to cry as she reached for him. But suddenly the vampire was there, and she cringed.

"When I grabbed you from him, I touched your throat. I did not do it on purpose, I swear to you, but I know now who hurt you." She watched his lips as he continued. "He will harm you no more, and I swear to you he has paid for what he's done to you and all the others. As his maker, I will make it my life to keep you from harm from him and the others that seek to find you. Of this I swear to you."

"They want me to change too." He shook his head at her. *"They will find me. They always do, and...and I'm so very tired of fighting them."*

"I would like to give you a gift. You do not have to take it, but it is my blood." She started to shake her head. "Please listen to me. It is a gift of life I offer you. They will not be able to bite you so long as I live. No vampire will, ever."

"My father said that's the way it works. You take in a vampire's blood and he will own you." Peter shook his head. *"Are you saying that when I take your blood, if I take it, that you won't own me body and soul?"*

"Nay, child, I will only be able to protect you as none other can. I'm old and very powerful, and the vampire that bit you is long dead. Your family, they are all vampires now, save you?" She nodded. "Then you will need me to protect you against so many. Your mate, too, will have my protection, because you know as well as I that if they find you, and as you said they will, they will use him against you."

"*They will kill him.*" Peter nodded. She looked at the man who'd only moments before kissed her so wonderfully. His wounds were healing; she could see that his lip no longer bled. When her family found her, they would use Brock to try to bring her in line. They'd done it before and had killed her one and only friend.

Peter helped her sit up, and Brock scooped her up off the floor. She was afraid to struggle against him, but held on to his neck as he took her out the back door and into a little apartment she'd seen earlier. He sat her on the room's only chair and held her hand as Peter came in behind him.

As they spoke to each other, she thought about her father. He had told her the last time he'd captured her that he would change her if it was the last thing he did. He said that they needed someone to care for them, to fetch and carry for them all, and it was her duty to do so. Her duty, he'd told her, was to find them food and lure it back for them. When she'd asked him what he meant, she was slapped.

"A human, you imbecile. Someone we can all have our meal from, and then you'll be responsible for getting rid of it. In exchange for you doing this, I'll make sure you have a place to rest. You owe me and your brothers for this." She asked him how she owed him and earned another slap. "You will be turned tonight when we rise. You'll be here when we wake, or so help me, Emma, I will make your change hard on you."

She believed him. He chained her to the wall and left her hanging there. It had taken her nearly all day to get loose, and when she did, she took as much money as she could find from the house—which wasn't much—and ran. She'd been running since that night eighteen months ago.

Chapter 4

Brock watched her as she lay on the little bed. Peter had gone to contact his maker and to tell Rayne what was going on. He wanted to join her in the bed, but also knew that right now she was as fragile as he'd ever seen anyone be. When she looked at him, he smiled.

"I wish that we had a way of communicating." She nodded at him and pulled out her pad. He walked to the bed and sat on the edge, and when she didn't move but continued to write, he leaned over her to see what she was saying. Her scent made him close his eyes.

He wanted to taste her skin. He moaned when she shifted on the bed and her breast brushed against his arm. When she didn't move, he slowly slid his hand up over her knee and held it there, waiting for her to make the next move. She turned to look at him, and he felt his blood heat.

"I want to taste you." When she continued to look at him, he moved slowly toward her shoulder and kissed her there. Her shiver made him nip gently at her flesh. Adjusting them so that she was facing him, he moved his mouth up and over her throat and over the scar until he could curl his tongue around the shell of her ear. He whimpered when she laid her hand over his thigh.

Wrapping his hand around hers, he moved it up his thigh to his groin, then over his erection. She watched his face as he lowered his mouth to hers. Laying her back on the bed, he rolled his hips between her thighs and rocked into her as he kissed her. Christ, she was as hungry as he was. Cupping her breast with his right hand, he lifted her against him with his left and rocked into her again and again until she pushed at his chest.

He waited for her to do something, anything. Feeling his heart pound in his chest and his cock throb with need, he would welcome whatever she did that gave him something of her. When she pushed him a little more firmly, he sat up from her but didn't leave the bed. Her hands were shaking as she wrote on a clean sheet.

"Your friends will be back." He looked at the note, then at her. Was she telling him that for now they couldn't do this, or that she wasn't going to even later? He looked at the door, then at her.

"I could lock the door." She smiled at him, and he started to stand when the damned door opened and Peter walked in. He stopped at the entrance and looked at them both.

"I'm sorry." Brock nodded because he knew that as much as he liked the big vamp, if he spoke now he didn't think what he had to say would be very nice. "I could...I suppose I could come back."

"Do what you need to do, Peter. We have the rest of our lives." At least he hoped so. Right now all he could think about was rolling her back on the bed and burying himself as deeply as he could and staying there. But he also knew that she was in trouble with a group of beings he had no way of beating on his own.

Peter sat down and looked at them both. When Em leaned back against Brock, he had to fight hard with his cat to not bite her. He had to tell them both over and over "soon," but he wanted her now. Finally, he licked along her shoulder, and that calmed them some, but they both were still seemingly pacing just on the edge.

"Can you calm him?" He shook his head at Peter's question. "He's not going to be happy when she takes my blood, and I would as soon keep my body parts just where they are if you wouldn't mind so much."

"He can smell her." Peter nodded. "What is it you have to do? And I'm not being a dick here Peter, but do it slowly so he can understand too. They're as aggressive as I am, and both my tiger and beast want her."

"I have to give you my blood, both of you. But until you mate with her, I will only go to her when she needs me. Em and I have a connection because of Jimmy." Brock knew who Jimmy was. He'd set up the labs that had been experimenting on beings and trying to change them into something they weren't.

"Give it to me first; that way if...Christ, he is pissed." Brock stood up abruptly and moved around the room. There was no calming them. When Peter went to stand by Em, he snarled at him. "Peter, walk away from my mate."

"I can't, and you know it. The way you are right now, you could scare her. She's already terrified, and if you'd just let him see that, he might calm." Brock felt his brother touch him, and he snarled at him to fuck off. "Brock, you're shifting."

He had to leave, but he couldn't leave her with Peter. When his cat started to get the better of him, he reached for Ryland and begged him to hold him. But he'd waited too long, and his beast took him.

Staring at the two of them through his cat's eyes, he watched as Em cringed away from him. Peter moved two steps closer to the bed, and he growled low. Brock moved to the other side of the bed and felt the moment that Ryland's cat, bigger and badder, reached out to his.

"Step back now." His beast lowered his body to the floor. *"Now or I'll punish you. Move away from the female or I'll hurt you."*

His beast snarled at him but did finally move back. His cat, the calmer of the two inside of them, roared too. Ryland kept talking to him, but all Brock could see was fear in Em's eyes. Peter finally stepped away from her, but Brock watched him.

"Brock, you have to control him or he's going to hurt someone." He snarled at Peter. "What's going on? This is more than me just touching her. What's happened?"

He wished he knew. He was so close to the edge right now that he was suddenly afraid for her, but his need to touch her was overwhelming. He crawled forward on his belly toward her, and when she didn't move, he heard Peter telling her not to make any sudden moves but to comfort the cat. Ryland was telling him to shift back, and he knew he should, but he didn't think he'd be able to.

When he leapt up on the bed, Brock laid his head on her thigh and watched her. She was staring at him so intently that he wasn't sure if she was upset or not. When she reached out her hand toward him, it was trembling. He lay very still, and when her hand touched him, he purred.

"Brock, move toward her, but slowly. She's not nearly as afraid as I am." Brock looked at the vampire. "I'm going to give you my blood this way, and then her. Then I'm getting out of here, if you don't mind."

Brock nodded and moved closer to Em. When she curled her hand into his fur, his cat calmed his beast a great deal. Peter moved toward them, and he didn't want to tear his throat out any longer. His brother Ryland laughed.

"You're going to have to explain to me what the fuck just happened. You're much calmer now, but, Christ, your cat was fucking irate." Brock agreed with him. *"Has that ever happened before?"*

"No and yes. I couldn't do anything but let him shift. It's like…I have no idea, but I knew that somehow if I didn't, I was going to hurt someone. The two of them are fighting to claim her." He smelled blood and looked at the wrist in front of him as Ryland asked what he meant by "the two of them." *"Let me get back to you after this. I promise I'll explain everything that I know."*

Peter held out his wrist that he'd cut open. Em's hand tightened in his fur, and he rubbed his head over her. When he licked the offered wound, he felt the connection to Peter snap into place, more so than even with his brothers.

"Christ." He agreed with Peter as he lifted his arm to Em. She looked at him, and he purred for her. When her tongue lapped at Peter, he felt his beast's anger once again, but nothing like before. When Peter stepped away from the bed, Brock didn't move.

"I'm locking the door on my way out. If you need me, either of you, I'll know. But as I said, she's a child of my child, and I'll go to her first. She's my responsibly more than you." He nodded. "I must go. I don't know what happened here, but…Brock, something happened more than you taking my blood. You know that, right?"

He nodded again and watched the man leave, shaking his head. There was something more, but he wasn't sure what it was, and it scared him a lot, more so that Peter didn't seem to know either. He looked at Em as she stared at him.

~~~

Em knew she should be afraid, but she wasn't. Not of him. He looked so large lying next to her in the tiny little bed. He raised his head and looked at her, and she knew he was trying to communicate with her. She wondered if he could read if she wrote it out for him. When she picked up her pad, he put his large paw over it and shook his head.

"*Hi.*" She felt Rayne touch her mind and smiled. The woman had so much humor in her voice that Em laughed back her greeting.

"*Brock has contacted me to tell you what he wants. He said for you to only do this if you want because he is in no hurry to scare you anymore.*" Em told her okay. "*He wants to know first, did he hurt you?*"

"No, he didn't. He...I was scared at first, but after he changed I...I was okay. He's very beautiful, isn't he?"

She waited while she knew that Rayne was speaking to him. When he lowered his head to her thigh again, she smiled and rubbed just behind his ears and felt his purr along her entire body.

"*He said you're more beautiful than anything he's ever seen. And so you know, I've told him that I'm not going to be repeating any romantic shit for him. He'll have to do that on his own.*" Em laughed, and Brock raised his head and looked at her. "*Brock is a good man, Em, and he only wants what you want to happen. That being said, the only way the two of you will be able to talk is if he bites you.*"

Her body stiffened, and she wanted to tell her no, but Rayne continued. "*You know that he won't hurt you, right? And if you know this, then you know that his bite will only mark you and not change you. He said he would never do that to you without your permission. And Em, he could do it without your consent or knowledge, but when he bites you, it will give the two of you a link that you can speak together like we are."*

"How is it that you and I can talk? Why can't he do the same?" She knew the answer before Rayne could tell her. *"Because you're not just a tiger, are you?"*

"No, and neither is Bronwyn. She's the female to this streak. In case you don't know what a streak is, I'll tell you. It's a family or a pack of tigers. And Ryland is the oldest, so he is considered the male. And, of course, Bronwyn is his female counterpart and a pain in my ass."

Em looked down at the big cat that had closed his eyes. She had no doubt that he wasn't sleeping but as alert to his surroundings as she was. When he opened one eye and looked at her, she asked Rayne if it would hurt.

"Not much. He'll lick the area first, and that will take away most of the pain, but it will hurt a little. He can bite you anywhere, but they prefer the shoulder. The left one because of how close it is to your heart, I think."

Could she let him bite her? She thought she could but wasn't sure. He was...he could have done so without asking, and as big as he was, he'd not have any problems holding her down while he did it either. She wanted to try.

"Tell him that...would you please tell him to do it?" Rayne said she would. *"And Rayne, I wanted to tell you thanks. You...you didn't have to do this."*

"I wanted to. As I said, Brock is a great man, and he's a wonderful protector. Even though I knocked him on his ass the first time I saw him." She laughed. Em knew the exact moment that he'd heard her answer from Rayne.

He leaned up and pushed his nose under her shirt. She wasn't sure what he wanted her to do until he licked along the exposed skin. She pulled her shirt up until it was just covering her breast when he nosed her again.

Okay, she thought, he wants it off me. She took her shirt off and covered herself with it until he pulled it from her with his teeth. Being half naked to him like this had her feeling very exposed. When he nosed her bra, too, she felt her toes curl up and watched his face as she stared at him. This was going to be a great deal harder.

He never took his eyes off her face as he pawed at her. Heart pounding, she reached down and unclasped the front closure on her bra and held it over her as he moved closer. Her body was burning up, and she tried to squeeze her thighs together to hide that she was also very aroused. But he put his other paw between her legs and prevented her from doing it.

When she let go of her bra, he licked her breast and took her breath away. Then when he moved his mouth to her shoulder, she wrapped her arms around him and held him as he ran his tongue over her entire throat and to her shoulder again. She shivered when he scraped his teeth along her. And when he sank them into her, she cried out, not so much from the small pain, but from the surprise of it.

"*Hold me.*" His voice sang through her mind, and she held him tighter to her. "*Hold me while I seal the wounds.*"

When he lifted his head from her, she looked up at him and rubbed her hand over his furred chest. While her fingers curled into him, she felt his body beginning to shift beneath her fingers, and watched as the cat seemed to merge into the man. As his mouth formed, he kissed her. His body, now fully a man, laid over her until he was covering her.

"*I want you with every breath I take. I can smell your heat and want to take you right now.*" She moaned when he rocked into her. "*Em, please say something.*"

"Take me." He lifted his head and looked down at her as she moved her hand down his chest to his waist and beyond. When he shifted for her, she wrapped her hand around his shaft and moaned again when he rocked into her. *"Please. I don't have...I've had sex, but I've never...I need you to help me know what to do."*

"If you had any more experience, I'd be a dead man right now." She smiled at him. *"If I enter you, take you, I'll mark you. And when I do, I'm going to bite you and claim you too. My cat is beating at me to just do it, but I want you to be sure this is what you want. We're moving very fast."*

She wrapped her legs around his thighs and rocked upward as she pulled him down to her mouth. Every part of her body wanted him to touch her, and she was pretty sure he'd get to that with her soon too. When she bit his lower lip, she tasted a slight coppery taste of blood and moaned. He cupped her ass, and she felt a moment of panic at remembering how large he was.

"I won't hurt you." She nodded and felt his hand slip down the back of her pants. *"But these have to go."*

The feel of her pants ripping made her rock up to him again. When he shifted his body, she felt for a moment that he was leaving her, but he pulled her ruined pants from her. Her panties were the only thing keeping them apart.

"I want to taste you until you come down my throat." She nodded, suddenly dizzy with need. *"And then when I've had my fill, I'm going to eat you again and again until you can't move."*

"Please." He moved down her body and took her nipple into his mouth and suckled hard. Every nerve ending in her body jerked to attention as he tugged at her other one. When he laved his tongue over the valley between her breasts, she curled her hands into his hair and

held him to her as he suckled at the other one. She rocked up to each of his downward strokes until she felt something racing over her quick and hot.

"*Come. Come, baby, so I can drink in your smell.*" She bowed up, not sure what was going to happen when her body exploded. Her climax had her grabbing for him to hold on, sure she was going to fly away. As he moved more down her body, she was trembling. He lifted his head as he suckled at her navel, and then when he rolled his tongue there, she moaned at him again.

"*Are you sure?*" In answer she wrapped her legs around his chest. "*I guess you are. I'm going to enjoy this. And I'm going to make sure you do as well.*"

His tongue entered her, and she nearly came apart again. As he moved his tongue in and out of her, she felt him enter her with his finger too. His mouth devoured her pussy; he ate at her lips and suckled her clit. Every time she was close to release again, he would back off and move to her thigh, nipping and kissing her until she was able to breathe again. Brock was making her wild for him, and when he moved to her clit again, she grabbed his hair and begged him to let her come.

"*Then come for me, love. Come hard and let me drink from you.*" She rocked upward and saw stars dance behind her lids as she let go. His growl made her think of his cat, and she came again, so lost in the thought that she nearly begged his cat to take her. As he began to make his way up her body again, she could see her cum on his mouth, his lips swollen from his intimate kisses. When he took her mouth, she felt his tongue dance with hers and she could taste her on him. When he was at her entrance, she moaned slightly and looked up at him.

"*I'm sorry, Em, but this will hurt.*" She nodded. Then she screamed in her mind the moment he pushed into her. The pain was incredible and tore through her as if he'd ripped her apart. When her mind seemed to calm, she realized he was speaking to her, soothing her with his hands as he did so. When she opened her eyes, just then realizing that she'd closed them, he wiped at her tears on her cheeks and kissed her gently.

"*I'm so sorry. I knew that you'd be tight for me and thought to get it over with quickly. I was so wrong. I'm so sorry.*"

"*I'm...it hurts, but not that bad.*" She tried to smile at him. "*You're very large, aren't you? Much bigger than —*"

He kissed her again and smiled at her. "*Never bring up past men to me. I would hate to have to go and hunt them down and kill them. And while we're on the subject of past men, I'm happy to say that none were larger than me.*"

She giggled silently in her mind, something she couldn't remember doing for a long time. When she shifted her body beneath him, hoping to show him how much she wanted him to move, she stilled when he did.

"*I'm going to roll to my back and take you with me. I want you to ride over me, but don't move until you're ready. This way you'll be able to take me as deeply as you want and....*" She shifted again, and he moaned. "*You keep that up and I'm not going to last until I get you above me.*"

When he rolled, she was suddenly sitting upright, and he was beneath her. She put her hands on his chest to adjust her legs and was shocked at how fantastic it felt like this. When she rolled her hips forward again, he put his hands at her hips and held her. She ignored his hands as he tried to hold her still and rocked forward again.

"*Baby, you're going to make me come before you if you keep this up.*" She moaned at him when he sat up. His cock was so deep in her, and when he sat up, he touched her clit in ways that had her wanting to take more of him. As soon as he suckled at her nipple, she wrapped her legs around him. He grabbed her ass and helped her lift up and down over his cock.

She was coming again, the speed of it running along her skin and veins so fast that she threw back her head and let it take her. He bit her again, this time deep in her shoulder where her arm attached. Leaning forward, she tasted his skin, licked the same path that he'd take until she was at the juncture of his neck and shoulder. His command to bite had her licking her lips to taste him. She sank her teeth down around his muscle and came so hard that she saw the darkness come up and take her.

Chapter 5

Gilbert Cole woke. He reached out to see what had disturbed his sleep and couldn't find anything wrong within his house, and nearly closed his eyes again when he felt her. His daughter, Emma…she had taken a mate. She'd fucking taken a mate without his permission.

He roared out his anger as he flew from his bed. How dare she? How dare she take a mate without his consent? He reached to her and knew that she was blocking him again. She had much to pay for when he caught up with her, and if what he thought had happened just now had, she was going to pay such consequences that she may beg him to change her from the pain he planned to inflict on her body.

Moving to the upper levels of their borrowed home, he found that his sons were still asleep, and that the one that had been hired to watch them while they rested was sleeping himself in the kitchen. He moved to this room without touching the floor, wanting to sneak up on the man and show him what happened to one that did not do as they were told. But he stopped just short of entering the room, knowing that the sun still shone in that room.

A memory came to him then, one from his own maker just before he left them this last time. "Do not kill those that watch your rest. They are all that comes between you and the sunlight."

Sage advice, but the man had fallen asleep and needed to be shown the errors of his ways. As he waited for the sun to lower enough to allow him to enter the room, he felt his sons begin to wake. Steven was first to rise and made his way to the upper levels, as Shawn and Erwin did a few minutes later. Wilfred was already gone from his bed, and Bert, as he'd been called most of his life, wondered for a moment if he had stayed out too late and had found the sun. Wilfred was not happy about the current arrangements. But then he was rarely happy anymore.

He wanted to kill everything that moved. Any and all humans, as far as he was concerned, should be food for them and nothing more. Bert, too, felt this way, but they'd been cautioned about killing where they lived. Drinking from the humans was possible, and actually the preferred method of living with them, but his sons and him, especially Wilfred, had wanted more and had killed several humans recently, and that had the authorities asking questions of everyone. It was much more fun to kill than it was to simply drink.

His son touched his mind just as the sun was low enough for him to enter the kitchen. Wilfred sounded as if he was drunk and Bert wondered about that. Alcohol couldn't hurt them, but it no longer gave them the buzz it had before.

"I've had the most fucking fantastic meal I've ever had." Bert felt his son's joy and was jealous of it, hot hatred jealous of it. *"You have had nothing until you've drunk from a shifter. And, Christ, they fight you for it. It's like...it's like a meal and a show."*

"Where are you? I demand that you come home this minute. The watcher sleeps instead of keeping us safe, and you're off killing." His son laughed, and he wanted to murder him. "Your sister has taken a mate. It's imperative that we find her before it's too late."

"Too late? I'm pretty sure if she's taken a mate, it's already too late. The fucking whore will have a kid in her belly, and we'll be shit out of luck before it's born." The drunkard feelings he'd gotten from his son had been replaced with hate. He'd never cared for his sister before they'd been changed, and now....

"What has she taken between her legs? A human? Another vampire?" Wilfred laughed bitterly. "She wouldn't take the last one we put there; what would she be doing with another one between her thighs? Not that it matters; whatever it is, he's a dead man. He just doesn't know it yet." Bert hated the way his son referred to Emma as if she were nothing more than a whore that had been born just to piss him off.

"I don't know what it is. Only that he's claimed her. It would have to be something other than human, wouldn't you think?" Wilfred didn't know either. "I wish that Jimmy were here. He could answer these questions instead of us trying to figure them out on our own."

They'd each felt the moment he'd been killed. They didn't know what had happened or what caused it, other than the profound grief that he'd been gone from their lives. It had actually taken them a week to figure out what they'd felt at the time, and it wasn't until they'd stolen into the library and looked up some information in a few books that they finally came to the realization that he was gone. Of course they'd been women's books, but that was all they could find. He was pretty sure that Wilfred had read them all. He went on for days how the vampires in the books he'd read had been portrayed as romantic and full of goodwill.

"I'm nearly there now. I think you're right. We need to step up our game and bring the bitch home. She needs to be changed like us and join the family or die. I'm sick of hearing about her and how she's gotten away." Bert agreed with him but said nothing. Emma had fooled them all enough. She'd gone along with them so willingly...well, not willingly, but she'd finally said she'd accept her duties and let one of them change her. Erwin had given her the idea to let her choose who it would be.

As soon as the door flew back on its hinges, the man from the kitchen came out. Bert had been startled so badly that he lashed out before thinking. As soon as his fangs sank into the man's throat, he knew his mistake. He'd been warned, and now he was feeling the raw pain of his blood filling his mouth.

It was hot and felt poisonous as it coursed through his body. He couldn't stop from drinking from him as he lifted his head, because the vein had been torn open, and his blood sprayed him in the face. The man clawed at him, his nails dug deeply into the flesh of his face and tore at him, but Bert was already staggering away. Even as the man dropped to the floor, his blood surrounded Bert's bare feet and burned him. Crying out, Bert lifted his body high from the floor, but it did him little good. He was burning; he was in so much pain that he was screaming over and over from it until he passed out from the pain.

When he woke, Bert didn't know where he was. His body ached, and he felt a hunger like none he'd ever known. When he looked around the bed, there were two women. One was tied to his bed post, the other to his bed, her hands and legs tied to the head and footboard.

"Drink from them so you can heal. You look like shit, Dad, and I can't stomach it much longer to be in this room with you." He looked at Shawn as he lounged in the chair. "Wilfred said to make you drink from them or he would end you. He's pretty pissed at you right now."

He looked at the woman who was tied to the bed. Christ, she looked delicious. His fangs dropped as his son moved toward them. He looked at Shawn as he opened his pants and jerked the one at the post to his cock. He could have her for now, but he was going to get his fill from them both. And this one was going to get the fucking of a life time while he was at it.

Pulling the sheet off her, he looked down at her nakedness. His cock thickened, and he leaned down and bit into her breast and let her blood fill his mouth. Her screams were muffled by the gag at her mouth, so he tore it off. Like Wilfred, he liked a show with his meal.

Her begging to be let go only made him harder. He moved between her legs and bit her again on her pussy. Her blood filled his mouth even as his tongue filled her. She was getting wetter. When she cried out, he lifted his head and looked at her, feeling her blood and cum drip from his mouth. Lifting her up, he tore the bonds from her ankles and rolled her over. Slamming his cock into her ass, he relished at her screams until he felt his balls tighten. When he lifted her up to his mouth by her hair, he sank his fangs into her throat and drank deeply of her.

Shawn cried out behind him, and he turned. He was coming all over the bitch that was his, and he snarled at him. As he pulled from the dying woman on the mattress, he moved to the foot of the bed and rammed his cock down the other woman's throat. He was deep, too deep for her to breathe, but he didn't care. She wasn't going to live long enough anyway for anything to matter. As soon as he felt her struggle less, he took her wrist and tore it open, spitting the flesh on the other body. He drank his fill of her as well. When a cock nudged his ass, he leaned over just enough to give Shawn what he needed. As soon as his cock entered his ass, Bert came hard down the woman's throat, and he held onto her post as he was fucked hard as she bled out.

Shawn leaned over him when he came, his teeth grazing his skin but not breaking it. They were of the same maker and didn't think they could feed from one another, but Christ, the things that Jimmy had taught them about sex and each other had gone a long way to them being sated more than they'd ever been. When Shawn pulled from his body, Bert did as well from the woman. Both of them would have to be taken care of, but for now he wanted to bask in his bliss.

"You're still marred up." He looked at Erwin, who had entered. "I guess that part of what he told us was true. We can't kill our watchers."

Bert went to the mirror and looked at his face. He'd been surprised the first time he'd seen his reflection and had said as much to Jimmy. He'd laughed at him for nearly ten minutes until Bert, in a fit of rage, had tried to attack him. He was frozen on the spot, not able to lift a hand against him.

"You can never harm me unless I have done you a great injustice. And other than making you all children of mine, I've done nothing to cause you harm." He'd told them that the house they were now staying in was his and would be until such time they were one hundred years young as a vampire. Then he would expect them to move out on their own. He also told them that there would be money for them to use as well. They never got to see any of that because he'd left them to their own devices shortly after that. That had been over eight years ago.

His face was marred in a new scar sort of way. Large scars made his cheek look like he'd had acid poured over it, and his hands and arms were no better. His feet were still tender and looked raw and ravaged. He turned to his sons.

"Do you think this will recede?" Neither of them would look at him, and he turned back to the mirror. He knew it wouldn't as surely as he was standing there. He saw Wilfred and Steven come into the room as he was pulling on a robe and Shawn was wrapping the women in the sheets from the bed.

"We will find her soon. I know that she's in Ohio somewhere because Jimmy had told me before when I contacted him about her. He said she'd stay there for a while before moving toward Florida. He thought she'd think she was safe in all the sunshine and we couldn't touch her." Wilfred glared at Steven when he snorted. "You have something to add, or do you want to stay here and wait for hell to break loose?"

"What do you mean?" Steven looked at him when Wilfred didn't answer him, and he shrugged. "Christ, Wilfred, what have you done?"

"How the fuck was I supposed to know who she was? She smelled good, and I was hungry. And her friends, too, smelled like sex and...." His eyes glazed over for a second. Then he looked at him. "At least I didn't kill our watcher. Now what the fuck are we supposed to do before we get Emma back here to fucking do what she's told?"

He'd killed nine teenagers, all of them from prominent families. The news had run nothing else since the bodies had been discovered. Wilfred had torn them up so badly that they were having difficulties identifying which body part went with the other. Bert discovered this when he went to the scene and witnessed firsthand his son's destruction. He watched as policeman after policeman went to the bushes and puked up their meals and then staggered away. Bert hadn't realized that Wilfred had such rage in him until that moment. They left before sunrise, moving to another town closer to Ohio. At this rate and the way Wilfred was acting, they would be lucky if they made it to Ohio. His son had gone over the edge and was quickly becoming a problem.

~~~

Jules sat down next to him, and Brock hugged him. They'd been late to the party, and he told him again how sorry he was. Jules told him not to worry about it.

"She's the reason you were late?" He nodded toward Em as she helped their mom set the table. "If so, then I have no choice but to forgive you. She's beautiful."

She was too. Her blonde hair was tied back in a pony tail that hung to her waist. She'd put other ties around it at different lengths to hold it, she'd told him. He'd been so mesmerized by watching her brush it out after they'd gotten out of the shower that he'd taken her back to bed and made love to her again. He needed to curb himself though. He knew she was sore.

"She's nervous about being around you all. She seems to think that one or all of you are going to pounce on her about her becoming my mate." Jules looked at him oddly. "She's a little insecure. Okay, a lot insecure. But if you knew her story like I did, you'd understand completely."

Jules laughed and handed him a package. He'd been handing them out since they'd gotten there. He took it and set it aside. He needed to ask him something.

"You've done some research on our history, right?" Jules nodded. "Something happened today that I don't...I think I even scared Ryland. I've always known that I have more than one cat in me. One of them I call the beast and he's very aggressive, but the other is my cat that I can control. The beast? Today I couldn't control him. I mean, at all. He took me, and no matter how hard I tried to hold him back, he wouldn't obey."

Jules looked at Em, then at him. "Who was with you? Her, I'm assuming, but whom else?"

He told him what Peter was doing there and what they'd done. Jules didn't speak for a long while, and Brock just let him run things through his mind. Jules was a thinker, and he was damned good at it. When he did turn to him, he looked confused.

"Let me talk to Keith. He has everything about our history downloaded on the computer. Maybe...let me talk to him first. But as I can see whatever it is, it's over, right?" Brock nodded. "I'll get back to you."

He stood up and went to Keith. Before he could protest that he didn't have to leave his party to look now, he was also worried that he felt compelled to do it right now. He reached for Em when she moved past him and pulled her into his lap. She looked up at him, and her eyes glazed over from need.

"You're not going to be able to walk if you look at me like that much longer." She kissed his mouth quickly and tried to stand. *"No. If you look at me like you're hungry, then you have to give me a proper kiss."*

"But a proper kiss to you involves a bed or shower and no clothes." He wiggled his brows at her. *"Behave or I'll tell your mother what we did in her driveway before pulling all the way up here."*

He growled low and nipped at her neck. *"You mean when you came in my mouth, or when I came in yours?"*

He'd had to have her and pulled over and laid her back on the seat of his truck and tore her panties off her. He was glad she'd had on a little skirt or he might have had to take her shopping again. Christ, he just couldn't get enough of her. When she tried to stand again, he let her. His mom was giving him the look that made him feel ten again.

When she sat beside him, he knew that he was either in big trouble or...hell, he was in big trouble. She wrapped her arm around him, and he kissed her forehead. When she didn't speak at first, he simply watched Ryland's little girl as she played with the toys that hung over her as she lay on the floor.

"Did you know that you're the only child I had that I couldn't control?" He looked at her. "When you were a child, even a baby, I was terrified you were going to get hurt. You did more often than not, but soon you learned to fall, and then more and more...or I guess less and less, you didn't need me following you around with a first-aid kit."

"I need you. I always will." He wrapped his arm around her just as she'd done to him. "Mom, I don't know if you heard or not, but I had a problem today."

"Ryland already asked me. And I don't know. He said that...you frightened him, I think. He said you'd been more wild tiger than you normally were, and that your human side was nowhere he could find in the cat's mind."

He nodded. That's how it had felt too. He was there, but not. The beast had dominated him.

"Jules and Keith are looking into it for me." She nodded. "I was…I've never been so terrified in my life. All I could think about was her and having her. I don't know what I would have done to her had Peter not been there, or Ryland roaring at me to come back."

"Long ago, there was a mated pair of tigers that lived among our streak. They were wild, not shifters like us, but they lived around us and even ran with us when the mood suited them. When their cubs were born, they had seven—too many for the young mother to handle—and the male brought us one to help with." He leaned back on the couch to watch her as she continued. "You were a baby at the time, and I had been in the kitchen when he came by. After he dropped off the kitten, I picked him up and held him until I realized that he wasn't coming back for him."

"Never?" His mom shook her head and told him when the cub was weaned he came back, and from time to time, the mother would as well to check up on him. "So what happened? You fed him?"

"Yes. I would pump my milk for him while I nursed you. He did so well that after a few weeks he was bigger than his siblings and much…smarter too. After three months and he was eating meat, the big tiger came back for him. A week later, there was a large stag on the doorstep, and one a week thereafter until…."

"Until what?" She looked away, then back at him, and he could see the tears in her eyes. Whatever had happened was not good; he just knew it.

"You were out playing and you fell. There was an abandoned mine on the property that we'd been warned about but had never encountered until then. You fell into it and broke your leg."

"He saved me. I remember thinking that it was Dad, but it had been the big tiger that we'd see once in a while. He shimmied his way down the long shaft and dragged me back out. He...he bit me on the thigh when he nearly dropped me." She shook her head, and he nearly told her he remembered.

"It was the cub that saved you, darling, not the father." He looked at her when she stood up. The cub had saved him? He stood up and started to ask her what that meant when it occurred to him.

"He marked me when he bit me." She shrugged her shoulders. "He did, didn't he? He marked me as his kind, and that has something to do with what happened today with Em."

"I honestly don't know. It could, I suppose, but...I really wish I could help you." He sat down and watched as Em walked around the rest of the table helping the caterer refill the trays of food that had been emptied. She smiled at him when she turned to him, and he fell in love with her. He looked at his mom and had a feeling she already knew.

"Ryland will help you protect her, as will Peter, but when her family comes here, they'll be as strong together as we are. And with them being vampires, they'll be faster, and I believe a great deal meaner than we will be." He nodded, knowing what she was saying was true. "Do you have a plan to change her?"

"I've not asked her. I'm not going to either, until this is over. I don't want her to feel pressured like I think she has been from her family. I think...I know they've tried that with her and it didn't work. I'm not going to make her feel that way." She nodded and smiled at him. "You think I'm wrong."

"On the contrary, I think it's the smartest move. She'll respect you more for it." He nodded and told her he loved her. "Of course you do. I'm the best mom in the world."

Brock laughed; there was no hope for it. She *was* the best mom in the world, and she was all his. He reached for her hand and kissed it, then went to find Em. He wanted to take her into a closed room and see if he could muss her up again.

Chapter 6

Bert walked the street trying to find a meal. He'd been out last night, too, and had been surprised to find the streets rolled up like the sleepy little town knew that they were out trying to find a good, hot meal. He looked in the window of the house that was lit up like a tree and saw people walking around and enjoying themselves. If one of them stepped out, he'd show them what enjoyment was. His fangs dropped when he saw a woman in a skin—tight dress walk by the window.

He wanted her to come out but hadn't yet learned the art of making humans listen to him. Wilfred had. He'd learned all sorts of neat tricks before any of the rest of them had. And Jimmy had been so proud of him. Bert wanted to find a stake and run his son through with it. He was fucking sick of his son and his superior attitude.

"Why don't you just shadow yourself and go in after her? By the time you killed her, we'd be long gone and no one would be the wiser." He didn't turn when he heard his son. Bert was afraid that he would be able to see the hatred on his face and know that he'd been thinking of killing him.

"I don't want her that badly where I'd have to be around so much human smell." He felt his belly lurch at the thought of what humans smelled like, and wondered if he had had the same noxious odor when he'd been human. "You can if you'd like. I'm just going to find a meal somewhere else. Someplace where it's a lot safer."

He started to move away and was suddenly lifted off the ground by Wilfred. He was holding him with nothing more than his two fingers pinched together, but nothing touching him. That was another trick his son had, the ability to levitate others and bring them to him.

"Did I say you could leave yet? Did I give you permission to walk away from me, to turn your back on me?" Bert grabbed at air to try and get loose. "You're not going to just walk away without having a little fun, are you, Daddy dear? You're that much of a chicken shit that you'd rather leave than play. There is so much sweet blood in that house alone that we could all feed well. Won't you join us?"

His other sons were suddenly there too. Erwin was wiping his mouth, and blood smeared over his lips. Bert felt his own fangs drop, and he could smell it on his son. Need coiled around him, and he looked at the window where the people were.

"We can't get in, but we can lure them out. Then we'll go in and make a feast for ourselves." Bert was dropped to the ground, and he snarled at Wilfred. "You'll keep a civil tongue in your head, Dad, or I'll be forced to rip it from you."

Bert had so many things he wanted to say, so many things that he thought about doing to the man his son had become. And none of them had anything to do with pride or love. His son had become a creature, an evil and unholy creature. And Bert was afraid of him.

As Wilfred barked orders to where the others were to wait, Wilfred moved to the window they been standing near such a short time ago. When the woman he'd been looking at came to the window, she leaned down and opened it, and Bert could see all the way to her pussy down the cleavage of her dress.

"Go to the door and open it. Then invite us in." She nodded and moved back, but Wilfred called her back. "You'll strip naked and be waiting for me. I'm going to fuck you until you scream."

She smiled at him and went to the door. Bert and his other sons were there waiting when the woman opened it. She was naked, and the people around her were staring. She moved to the threshold and invited them in. As soon as the words spilled from her lips, Wilfred took her to the floor and bit into her throat.

The screams started almost immediately, but as quickly as they started, they were cut off. As Bert moved to a man who was shielding the woman he was near, he looked him in the eye and told him to take out his dick and masturbate. As soon as he tore open his pants, Bert grabbed up the luscious women he'd been protecting and tore her clothes from her. He was fucking her in the ass when the man came.

"Again." He watched the man fist his cock over and over. He was in pain, Bert could see that, but he didn't care. The woman beneath him tried to get away from him, and he reached down and broke her neck as he came in her.

As the guests were killed off, he could see his sons feeding on the few that still lived. Shawn was eating one woman and had one riding him. He could hear him slurping at her, and he felt his cock harden again. One thing he'd learned about being a vampire was that he was never satisfied when it came to sex. Drinking from the half-naked man as he shot his second load over the dead woman, he dropped him to the floor, not even bothering with closing the wound. He stepped to the two maids that had been brought from the kitchen by Steven.

"Sharing?" His son nodded, and he could see blood staining his teeth. Bert took the younger woman and Steven the other. As he was drinking from her while he fucked her tight pussy, he felt someone come up behind him. Never one to turn down a good fucking, he spread his legs and moaned against the woman's throat when someone entered him hard.

The powerful thrusts he was giving the woman were now doubled, and when he came, he lifted his head from her throat and rubbed her blood over her breasts and bit her there. She was dying anyway, and he wanted to get as much as he could from her. The man behind him grabbed his dick as soon as he left the woman's cooling body and helped him jerk off as the man came inside of him. When he turned, he'd been terrified to see Wilfred there.

"Come again. I want to feel you release in my hand again." Wilfred fisted his cock tighter, and he felt the pain all the way to his balls. When he came a few seconds later, he was afraid to think about how he'd done it. He was afraid that his son had a power over him too.

Wilfred walked out the front door and commanded them to make sure there was no one left to tell. They searched the house from top to bottom, only finding one still alive, and Shawn had taken care of him. Snapping his neck, he left him among the bodies of the other fourteen guests and hired help, and laughed.

"We should do this more often. A family that feeds together stays together." Bert shivered, remembering something that Jimmy had said about nests. He nearly said he thought they should split up before they were all caught when he looked around and saw Wilfred standing there.

"You do it and I'll have no problem killing you." He asked him what he was talking about. "You know. We'll stay together or else; and when we get Emma back, there'll be no keeping her for our rest. She'll be fully changed and in my bed. I'm going to fuck a child in her belly."

"You know you can't have a child with her. She's not your mate and without that, there will never be a child from the two of you." Bert backed up when Wilfred advanced to him. "You know what I say is true."

"Then she has no use for us after I fuck her, so I'll kill her." Bert felt his skin tighten and his blood, at first hot and coursing through his body, chilled. The way that he'd said it, the way that Wilfred had said he would kill her, made Bert almost feel sorry for his daughter. Then he remembered what she'd done to them before she'd left. She'd tried to kill them by having the house set afire. That for a vampire was an unforgivable act against them.

Bert walked out of the house with his sons and watched when the police showed up. Wilfred had said he'd called them and they hung around to watch the show. And it was a show. They had no more idea what had happened than why. They did stumble around like they might have a clue, but whenever any of them mentioned vampires, one of them would change the direction of his thoughts.

As the sun started to crest the sky, they went to the lair they'd found and into the cellar. It wasn't the best of accommodations, but they were safe from the sun for another day. He thought about Wilfred's command to find Emma when the sun set and wondered just how they were supposed to do that. But sleep claimed him, and he felt his body, by slow degrees, shut down. He'd find her, but he wasn't so sure he'd let Wilfred kill her. He wanted her to be their watcher more than he wanted her dead. She owed him. She owed them all for what she'd done.

~~~

"Nineteen confirmed dead, and the police are still looking for clues. If anyone has any information on the murders in—" Em turned off the television and stared at the blank screen. She knew who it had been as surely as she was sitting there. She looked up when Bronwyn walked in.

"It's them, isn't it?" Em nodded. "That means they're less than four hundred miles from here. So at the rate they're traveling and the mayhem they're leaving behind, they might be here as soon as three days."

"Less." Neal sat down next to her and smiled. "How you holding up, sweetheart? Do you need anything before I go?"

She'd been staying with Alistair and his wife since the story broke. Brock thought he should go to the scene and see what he could find out, and had asked her to stay there while he was gone. He'd been afraid for her and she had told him she'd be fine. Now she wasn't so sure she'd ever be fine so long as her family was still alive.

"I wish I could help you." Alistair nodded and stood up. He was helping her teach the others sign language. "There are others around the yard. When you go out, make sure that someone knows you're out so that you aren't startled. Max has come to help watch you."

She'd met the large man. He had told her that he was a bear, and she believed him. She had never met a werebear before, and had been surprised to learn that nearly all species had a were counterpart. Even snakes, she'd been told, but they were harder to recognize as a shifter than others were. Brock had told her he thought it was because they were so small that no one noticed the scales. She'd laughed with him for twenty minutes.

After he left and Ally went to the Pretty Flower to work, Em tried to find something to do. The cook, Roland McBride, had asked her if she was hungry, but she hadn't been so much as bored. It was hard not doing anything after working for so long. She went back to the office that Brock had told her she could use and pulled up the Internet.

She was still doing some digging when the computer suddenly showed Keith's face. She watched as he typed across the screen. She smiled at him.

"I thought you could use this program. It's for deaf people so they can communicate better. You should be able to type back to me. Can you try?"

"How are you?" She clapped her hands when he gave her the thumbs up. "You are very nice to do this for me. I wasn't sure how I could speak to anyone that I don't have a link to."

"You should be able to talk to anyone, but not everyone will have a camera. And that might be a good thing." She laughed. "I have some news for you. It's not bad, but I already spoke to Brock, and he said I could tell you. What do you know about weretigers?"

"Nothing." She hit enter before continuing. "I know what I have heard from you all and some things I'd learned just by being around my family. Why? What have you found out?"

Brock had told her that his brothers were looking into what might have happened the day that Brock had bitten her. She rubbed her hand over the scar at her shoulder and waited while Keith continued typing. She didn't really care what had happened, but she knew that Brock had been scared.

"In our history there was a weretiger that had taken a wild tiger for his mate. The story goes that the two of them met when he'd been on a run and had fallen in love. And as you know how stories go, there was an evil father involved. The man's father, Benton was his name, had forbade his son to see the tiger again. He told his son that if he continued seeing her that he'd have his hunters find the female and kill her and have her skin put in the front hall of their home to remind him never to disobey him again."

She read the story as Keith typed more. "The son was so much in love with the tiger that he wanted to change her. He wasn't sure if it would work or not, but he thought that it would work the same way as it did with other species. Just biting during sex should do it. Or so he thought."

"Please tell me that the father didn't kill her. I'm going to be very pissed at you if he does." Keith looked at her in the camera and winked.

"No, but things didn't go well for the change either. Once the son bit the female to change her, something happened and he changed instead. He felt his body morph, and even though he had already shifted to a tiger, he shifted again...to a wild one that still had the feelings and knowledge of the man he'd been. It took him several days to fully convert, and when he was changed, he looked at himself in the pond near his home and saw that other than his eyes being a brilliant green, he was the same as he'd always been. He decided to go and see his father."

She held her breath, waiting for the story because she knew that something bad was going to happen even though he'd told her it wasn't bad. When he looked at her when he finished telling the story, she almost didn't want to read it.

"His father didn't know he was any different and yelled at him for coming into the house as a cat. He told his son then that he'd found him a mate that would bear him children and he'd forget the nonsense with the tiger. As he stood before the son, he noticed that he was different and dropped to his knees to beg him to tell him it wasn't true. His son left the home he'd grown up in and lived with his mate. It was their child, a human-born child, that started our family. A human child born of two wild tigers."

She read the last line three times before she looked at him. The hair on her arms danced as he starting typing again. She wanted to close the connection; she wanted to tell him she didn't want to know any more when he looked at her again. The words on the screen seemed to scream at her to read them.

"Every few generations a child is born that is stronger than the rest. He is bigger than his siblings, as well as more aggressive. They are always male, and they usually end up being the enforcer of the streak, or at times the male. And according to the story, this male never finds his mate. And if one ever did, the teller of this tale believes that they will breed a cat that will be a ruler of our kind."

He told her to open the file he sent her, and she shook her head. "Please, Em. I need for you to tell me if this is the cat that Brock became when he shifted that day. I need you to tell me if you saw anything like this in Brock.

The first picture was that of a man. He looked like he could have been Brock's twin but for his size. Brock was taller and much wider. The next picture was of a tiger, and her breath caught when she looked at him. She looked at

Keith, who was only half there because the picture had taken up that much of the screen. She nodded once.

"I knew it." He smiled at her. "I just knew it. Brock is that cat. He's the only one in all our history who has ever found his mate. Christ, Em, do you know what that means?"

"It means that Brock is meant for greatness." He nodded and smiled at her. She nodded back and told him she had to go. He was still typing when she closed the computer. Em was suddenly more afraid then she'd ever been.

Moving through the house, she ended up in the kitchen again. As she sat down, a glass of tea appeared in front of her and she looked up at Jules. He smiled at her and took a pad of paper out of his pocket and began writing. She couldn't think and most certainly didn't want to speak to him.

"I came by to see if you wanted to go to my studio." She frowned at him, and he took back his pad. "I have a large studio near here and wanted to see if you wanted to hang out with me. I have a few things to pack up and send out to some buyers, and there are a dozen people running around like...come with me?"

She had an idea that he was an artist but was not really sure what he did. There were flyers in Brock's den as well as Alistair's, but she'd never touched them after seeing Jules's name on them. As he led her out to his car, she wondered if she should ask him and decided that it didn't matter. She had to make sure that Brock was safe, and having her family so close was not a good thing. When they pulled up in front of a large metal building with several cars out front, she almost asked him to take her back. She didn't want to be around people right now. But he opened her door for her and helped her out. She walked behind him as he moved to the door. She would only stay for a few minutes, she promised herself, and moved into the building as soon as he opened the door.

The place was much bigger than it looked. She entered and was immediately struck by how clean it was. The desk was manned by a woman who looked like she could lift small cars by herself. He introduced her as Max the Bear's wife. She took her hand when it was offered and felt a small connection form. Before the woman could say anything, if she was, Em found herself being moved into a large open area that was simply chaos.

But the more she watched the people move, she thought it was more of a dance. One where the product, whatever it was, moved from one side of the room where she couldn't see it to the other where two men were forming wooden boxes around it. She was moved once, and then when someone moved her again, she pressed herself against the wall and stared. Jules handed her another note.

"They're packing my pottery up for a show that's coming up in a few weeks. This stuff is going to New Orleans for one of the largest shows I've ever done." He handed her another flyer, and this one told the reader that J. L. Golden was going to be the premier show caser, and that tickets were still on sale. He took it from her when she pointed to the ticket price, and he marked through it and wrote, "sold out." She smiled at him, and felt very proud to know such a famous person.

He took her arm, and she noticed that like the other men she'd come in contact with, he was careful only to touch her clothes. She'd asked Rayne about that and she said it was easier to wash out their scent from the clothes than it was their skin. She said that Brock, like all the others in the streak, were very protective of what they considered theirs. She said that few if any other males would touch her without asking Brock first...unless, of course, they wanted to die or wanted to piss him off. Brock had been doing it to her and Neal for weeks now, Rayne told her.

"Every time he comes near me, he would touch my neck or my face. Used to piss Neal off to no end every day. But now that I think about it, he's not done that...." Rayne smiled. "Not since you and he bonded, he hasn't. I guess I owe you something. Not that I didn't enjoy being marked by Neal every night, but he was getting to be a tad more aggressive about it."

Jules took her into a smaller room and showed her some of his work in process pieces. She recognized his design and marveled at the larger pieces that he still had to finish. He wrote her so many notes that she was sure he was getting tired of telling her everything and wrote that to him.

"Are you kidding? I'm having a blast. My family is bored with me bringing them out here to show them something. Having someone who's never seen my work is refreshing." She nodded at him and smiled. "Besides, Brock will be pissy when he comes back and smells me on you. Neal asked me to take over with you what Brock was doing to Rayne. It's more fun than I thought it would be."

She shook her head when he pulled on her ponytail and then ran his hand down her arm. She knew what he was doing and thought if the man wanted to play with fire, who was she to stop him? When he put his cell phone to his ear, she wandered away. A few minutes later, he touched her arm and all his humor was gone. She waited for him to tell her, but he only handed her the phone. Not sure what to do with it, she looked at it and nearly fell over. It was her father and Shawn coming out of a house covered in blood. She watched his mouth as he took back the phone.

"I think she knows them." She nodded. "She does. Hang on, let me see if I can find out. Can you give me their names for the police where this was taken?" She took out her own pad and wrote down their names. She knew it was from Brock and wanted to ask Jules if he would tell him to come home to her. But she knew that if he did, he'd tell her to stay and she had to let him become great. And being great with her around wasn't going to happen.

Jules read the name of her brother and father. He nodded once and closed his phone. When he opened it a few seconds later and handed it to her, she thought it was going to be another picture. He mouthed "Brock" and she looked down at the screen.

"I love you," it said, and she started to cry. "I will be home tonight. I miss you. And want to hold you."

"I miss you too and...." She wasn't sure if he really loved her or not, but she typed the words on the tiny keyboard. "I love you as well. But your brother said you are deemed for something special. I should go before it's too late."

"I will only be special with you by my side. I cannot—*will* not—live my life without you beside me. I love you, Emma Cole, and when I get home, I'm going to show you just how much."

She felt her body react to his statement and hoped he meant what she thought he did. She glanced up at Jules as he talked with the woman from the desk. When she looked down at the keyboard again, she nearly fumbled it.

"Will you be my wife?" It appeared twice more before he typed her name with several question marks. Before she could think out to answer, he touched her mind.

"*Marry me.*" She nodded and realized he couldn't see her, and told him she'd think about it. When he growled, she laughed, and suddenly she felt his touch along her skin like he was standing next to her.

"*Marry me, and when you say 'I do,' I'll take you into our backyard and let you run naked in the woods while my cat hunts for you.*" She moaned. "*Christ, baby you have no idea how much I want you right now.*"

"*Not nearly as much as I want you here now. Hurry home, Brock. I need you here with me.*" He asked her again if she'd marry him. "*Yes; if you still want to marry me after my family leaves, then yes, I'll marry you.*"

She felt his love wrap around her, and she knew that he really did love her. She handed Jules back his phone. He took her to his wheel and showed her how he made his art, but she was only about half paying attention. She was thinking up all the ways she was going to welcome Brock home. And what a home coming it would be.

Chapter 7

Brock decided to drive by the site that the boys were supposed to clean up on his way home. He pulled in and knew that it was a mistake, and actually almost went home to do it in the morning. But he was there and got out of his truck and walked to the building.

The lights on the second floor startled him, but the smell of ammonia had him sneeze twice before he could stop it. Moving up the stairs, he pulled out his gun and held it to his side as he moved to the room where the lights were.

Someone was scrubbing the walls. Brock stepped into the room cautiously and saw that while the kid was alone, he had a set of headphones in his ears, and even from where he was standing ten feet away, he could hear it blasting in the kid's head. He watched as the kid scrubbed at the blood on the wall.

What was written there now was new. The statement that had been put there before was on the wall closest to him and that wall was cleaned of the blood. He tried to read what it might have said and all he could see was a few words, but he got the meaning. More crap about the underdog and persecution. When the kid—Donny he realized his name was—bent to dip his rag in the bucket, he must have seen Brock because he jumped back and fell against the wall. He pulled the headphones out immediately.

"I was working on getting it cleaned up like you said." Brock nodded but didn't put this gun away just yet. "They said they were going to keep it up until...I don't want to go back there."

"Back where?" Brock moved into the room. In addition to the cleaning supplies he'd brought the first day they were to start the job, there was a sleeping bag and some clothes. He looked at the boy.

"They kicked me out. My dad said that if I wanted to be a goody-two-shoes, I had to do it without living under his roof. They must have come here today while I was at school and put more blood on the walls." Brock put his gun away but didn't put the safety over the handle.

"How long have you been staying here?" He told him four days. "And they know you're here?"

"Yes, sir. My dad said that no son of his was...I was going to leave when you okayed what I'd done. I don't know where yet, but I was going to go." He looked at his things, then at him again. "You think it would be okay if I stayed another night? I swear to you I won't do anything to harm your building."

Brock looked at the wall that had been painted with blood before. It was about as pristine as he'd ever seen it. Even the rug surrounding the area had been cleaned pretty well, and there were three large trash bags sitting next to the door. He looked back at Donny.

"Did your brother help you at all? I mean other than repainting the walls with pig's blood?" Donny shook his head. "I want to help you kid, I really do. I know your dad is having some problems, but kicking out his own son goes over the line. Especially when you were ordered to do something by law that…you had nothing to do with the wall in the first place, did you?"

"I was here, but no, sir, I didn't do anything." He started picking up his things. "I'll come by after school tomorrow and finish up. You might want to put someone here to watch it. I don't think they're finished—"

The noise in the lot alerted them. Brock put his finger to his lips and waved Donny into the corner where it was darkest. Brock went to the other side of the door and waited for the Owens to come up the stairs. He had no doubt who it was. While they were seemingly staggering up the stairs, he reached for Ryland to tell him what was going on and that he had someone there with him.

"You need to call the police and send them to the building on Decker. The vandals are at it again. And tell them I'm on site." He asked if he needed him to come there, he and Bronwyn were close. *"If you wouldn't mind coming in behind them, I'd like that. The more the merrier I think. But tell Bronwyn that we do this my way and not hers."*

She touched his mind then, and he felt her laughter. *"You think I would do anything less? Shame on you, Brock. I thought you knew that I have your best interest at heart."*

"I do. But there's a good kid with me, and I'm afraid for him. Can you, I don't know, use your powers for good and protect him? He's human." She told him she would and also told him that she was going to kick his ass.

Harvey came through the door first. He was drunk. And when his son walked in…fell in actually…Brock knew that he was drunk as well, and both men were carrying bottles of beer. Junior called for his brother and snickered when he found the cleaning supplies. He tossed them to the bloodied wall as he spoke to his dad.

"Our little housewife has been busy again. Should we help him keep working, or do you think that we should trash the place and him too?" Junior laughed. "I think we should find him a good husband so they can live happily ever after, like that shit he's always reading about. Who the fuck is he fooling reading those books anyway?"

"They're not fairy tales. They're mythology, and most of them ended in tragedy. You should leave before the owner shows up. He might be mad at us again." Donny kept his distance, but Brock was still afraid for him. The kid had balls, he'd give him that.

"I have him. Brave kid. And he didn't give you up. You think he's working on something?" Brock told Bronwyn he thought he was. *"Then let him do it. Might help him out too. The boy has some major self-esteem issues."*

"You think I give a flying fuck what the owner has to say to me? He fucking fired me without reason. He took away our house and our livelihood." Harvey advanced on Donny but didn't touch him. "You think I like living like we are, with no money and having to rely on welfare to survive?"

"Yes." Brock nearly laughed out loud when Donny answered him. "You and Junior spend all the money that comes on that card every month. You have money for beer and drugs when you want them, even though there's no food in the house anymore. And just last month you bought that car from Dino. How did you do that?"

"You think we don't have our resources? Hell boy, where do you think we get it? We been robbing the rich and keeping the profits. Them Goldens don't have a clue that we been getting in that storage building there on Tenth for months now and taken what we want." He started toward the wall that Donny had been cleaning. "I told you not to clean this here art up. I even told you what would happen if you did, didn't I?"

"The police said we had to do it or go to jail." His dad looked at him. "I don't want to go to jail again. They aren't nice to you."

"They're not supposed to be, you idiot." Junior sneered at his brother. "For all your smarts you're pretty fucking stupid."

"Hum, Brock, the police are on the lot and waiting. Do you think you have enough to get their asses hauled off to jail yet?" Bronwyn laughed. *"Ryland is ready to adopt the boy, by the way. And Alistair is on his way too. He seems to think he has something more to add to the already overpowering evidence to convict these idiots. Oh, and Em is coming with him. She was worried about you, and I told her that you were on a hot case."*

He'd gotten so wrapped up in this, he'd forgotten to call her. He reached for her now. *"I love you. And I'm so sorry."*

She laughed. *"I love you as well. And you really messed up this time. I was naked and waiting for you."*

His cock hardened and nearly took him to his knees. *"Em, you're going to pay for that. I'm working here, and I have a hard-on so bad right now that I can hardly think about anything but burying it in you so deep you scream out my name."*

"I was planning on that, too. I even went into town and got some silk scarves. Rayne showed me where to shop. I got us a few other…toys to play with too. Are you going to be much longer?"

He was a dead man. Growling at her had her giggle, and he nearly told Ryland to fucking forget it, that he was going to find his mate and take her. But he heard something that made his cat stir.

"You know them others that what's been coming around, Donny? They said that if we help them get that new bitch at that fucking flower shop that they'd give us riches we'd never spend in two lifetimes." Junior nodded when Donny shook his head. "They got fangs, too. Did you hear me? Fucking fangs, and they said that if we got her, they'd make us like them."

"*Bronwyn, are you — ?*"

"*I heard, and I'm calling in your brothers. And Alistair and Em are going to the main house now and not here. She'll be safe there, and Neal is headed that way, too. Your mom is with Gabriella, and they're aware that she's coming. Don't move…Brock, I can feel your cat. He's being pissy again.*"

He felt him, too. He was trying to take him again, and Brock was losing the battle. His skin began to burn with the need to shift, and his canines began to drop. He worked feverishly to get his gun in his holster so he wouldn't drop it. Then Em spoke to him.

"*I love you. Think of me in our bed. I had plans…I had plans to tie you to it and have my way with you.*" He asked her for more. "*I bought this cute little outfit that has barely any material to it at all. It was really expensive, but all I could think about was having you tear it from me. Shredding it into ribbons while you held me down on the bed. Then when you bent me over the bed and took me, I was going to play with my nipples and…and then I was going to take your cock into my mouth. Would you fuck me that way, Brock?*"

His cat snarled at him, but he could control him now. The more she talked, even if none of it was really making sense, he could feel his beast back down. His hands still trembled, but he no longer felt the need to kill. He felt Ryland touch his mind, and he told him he was fine to come on up, and suddenly the room was filled with cops.

~~~

Em paced the kitchen of the main house. She'd been there once before but wasn't really thinking of this as a social visit. The others in the room seemed to be talking, but for the life of her, she couldn't think of what they were saying. She turned to look at Rayne when she touched her arm.

"He's fine." She nodded. "*You probably saved his life by what you did tonight. Had he shifted when he did, the police would have shot him without a doubt. How did you know what to say to him, and do we want to know what it was?*"

She flushed, wondering where what she'd said to Brock had come from. She'd bought herself the outfit, but for the most part, she figured she'd just show it to him and that would be enough. As for her wearing it, she wasn't sure she'd be that brave. As for the rest, she was just saying whatever she could think of to get him to calm down. She looked at Rayne.

"*He was having trouble controlling his animal. It wasn't like the last time he brought him out, but like the very first time. He was…not meaner, but more like he didn't care what happened to him so long as…I guess so long as I was safe.*" She looked at Sandra. "*She said it's because of the baby that was born long ago. She thinks that Brock has some of him in him.*"

"*Probably. I heard the story too. And I wouldn't doubt that somewhere along the line Brock picked up more than his share of him. And finding you is what kept him from getting hurt. You're the first mate of any of the others. Because of you, he didn't end up like his ancestors – dead because he shifted at the wrong time.*" She smiled at her. "*You should really learn to play poker. There isn't a tell on you when you speak. For anyone looking at you, they'd think you were as serene as hell. But I know that there is all this panic going on in your head.*"

"What do you mean?" She looked around the room and wondered what they were saying about her. "*They think I'm not worried about him? I am. He's everything to –* "

"*We can feel your fear and anxiety. Humans? Never. Maybe not even other supernaturals. But you look as calm as if you're reading a boring book, and nothing is written on your face. That will be helpful when you have to deal with your family, I think. A sort of scary power that you can use against them."* She asked her what she meant. *"They're going to come here. We all know that, you more than others. But they expect you to be afraid, terrified even, because they think they're going to take you back with them. But you can stand there and pretend it doesn't matter to you one little fuck, because really, it doesn't matter. Don't you see? No matter what they say to you, you can make them think you just don't give a flying fuck. And that will piss them off. And pissed off beings are sloppy beings. And that, my dear sister, is when we're going to get them."*

Em thought about that after Rayne left her to sit at the table. She'd always been able to piss her family off when she'd pretended not to understand them. Even when she lived at home, the only one that had ever made any attempt to learn sign language was her mother, and she'd only done what she needed. Mostly commands, like set the table, shut up, and leave me alone. She looked at the people around the table fussing over the little baby, who was smiling.

Not one of them had ever done anything but make her feel welcome. Sandra had asked her to teach her how to talk to her, and Bronwyn had even asked her to teach her and Gabriella as well. She said that since she was going to be a part of this family, everyone, including the children, should learn to talk to her. She looked at Roland when he touched her arm. He handed her a large glass of tea and a plate. That was another thing she'd never been in her life—so full.

They were forever eating, but no one seemed to get heavy from it. Brock had told her it was because as cats they burned a great deal more energy than humans did. But she wasn't a cat and he had bitten her on the shoulder and told her that she was burning energy other ways. Then he proceeded to show her how. Christ, the man was a sex machine. She giggled to herself.

She loved him. More than she could explain to him, but she did try. When she touched him, he would smile at her, and she'd melt. When he kissed her nose, she felt as if he'd handed her a diamond. And when he made love to her, she'd never felt so cherished or loved by anyone. She looked down at the glass, and when she realized someone was tugging on it, she looked up at Roland.

"You want a refill?" She hadn't even realized she'd drank it, and apparently had eaten everything on the plate as well. "I have more."

She told Roland no but thanked him. He nodded at her and took the plate as well. She knew in that moment that she could never leave there. As much as she thought they'd be safer without her around, she couldn't leave. She decided it was time to speak to Rayne.

"Will you tell them something for me?" She nodded. *"Tell them that I have never been happier than I am right now. And for as long as I live, I will never be able to explain to them or repay any of you for what you've done for me. Tell them that I love you all so very much."*

Sandra got up first and hugged her tightly. Then Rayne. Roland even hugged her, and she heard from Ryland too. He told her it was his duty to love her, but she made it easy for him to do so. She laughed as they all told her that she was very special to them. And Keith told her that so long as she kept Brock as happy as he seemed to be right now, she was aces in his book. She looked at Rayne when she realized that she could speak to them all now.

"I was surprised by that myself. Something else to add you your awesome sauce list that grows daily." Em wasn't sure she could take too much more of anything that involved an

awesome sauce. She wondered if it went well with spaghetti and laughed. Sometimes learning new words was fun.

Em was holding the baby when she felt Brock getting close. She looked at the door and waited for him to open it. She could feel her heart begin to pound hard in her chest, and when someone took little Gabriella, she stood up. As soon as the door opened and he stepped in, she leapt into his arms.

He held her as she rained kisses over his face. When he took her mouth with his, she moaned and felt as if she could make it now. He lifted his head and grinned at her.

"I could get used to this, but I don't think my family will. Ryland is jealous that Bronwyn has never met him at the door this way." She looked around the empty room. *"They left before I kissed you. Christ, I missed you."*

"Let's go home." He nodded and turned with his arms still wrapped around her, and headed out to his truck. She was kissing his throat when he pressed her against the hood of his truck and rocked into her.

"We're not going to make it if you don't stop now." She nipped at his skin. *"Baby, you nearly killed me twice tonight. If you don't want me to take you right here, I would beg you to stop now."*

She didn't want to stop now. And more than that, she wanted him to take her in the woods like he'd been telling her he would for days now. She looked at the tree line and back at him. He glanced behind him, then at her. She nodded, and he sat her down on her feet.

"Do you want me to hunt you like prey?" She nodded at him. *"I'm going to be my cat. You understand that, don't you? He's very...very aggressive, and may not wait for me to shift all the way before he bites you."*

She smiled at him. *"Will it change me? Will it make me a cat like you if he bites me? I'd like that very much. I want you to make me yours in all ways, Brock. Now, tonight, I want you to change me. Would that be all right with you?"*

He didn't ask her if she was sure. She thought he might, but he didn't. He just took her hand and led her to the other side of the truck and opened the door. She was so disappointed that she grabbed his arm to ask him why.

"We're doing this at our home so that when you shift the first time, I can take you to the ground and roar out my release. I'm going to change you the moment we get home, and then I'm going to fuck you until you can't move." He kissed her hard on the mouth. *"There will be no going back after this. You're mine, and no one touches what's mine."*

He got in under the steering wheel and gripped the wheel so tightly that she could see his knuckles as they turned white. He looked over at her, and she could see his cat trying to surface. When she reached out to touch him, he grabbed her hand and held it.

"You touch me and I'll take you now." She nodded. *"Let me...I can smell you. He can smell you and wants you right now. Just...please don't touch me or I might...he might hurt you."*

Nodding, she put her hands in her lap and sat still. She could feel how close he was and wanted to comfort him, but knew if she tried the same trick from earlier, there would be no stopping him. And as much as she wanted him to take her, she didn't want him to change her in a truck. When they pulled in their driveway, he told her to get out and strip. She slipped out of the truck and smiled.

Christ, she was going to enjoy this.

Chapter 8

Brock was barely hanging on, and he knew the moment she was standing before him naked he was going to take her. He looked at her in the light from the house as she took off her shirt. He moaned when she leaned over, presenting her ass to him while taking off her shoes. He took off his own shirt as he watched her. Both his beast and his cat snarled at him to strip her now, but he waited for her.

Next, her bra came off. As she turned to him, she ran her hands over her breasts and cupped them. He reached down and freed his cock as he held onto the steering wheel. If she wanted to tease him, he was going to let her.

She unhooked the closure of her pants and left the material hugging her around her hips. He licked his lips when he thought of taking her breasts into his mouth and suckling them. When she bent to remove her pants, her breasts bounced slightly and he moaned and wrapped his hand around his engorged shaft. Precum made the slide much easier. When she dipped her fingers into her panties, Brock had had enough and opened his door, took off his pants, and tossed them into the truck.

"*You're beautiful.*" She never stopped moving her fingers along her pussy. "*Are you wet for me? Do you have juices enough to share with me? Or are you going to make yourself come for me and feed me?"*

She nodded and held out her fingers to him. Taking them into his mouth, he moaned at the taste and sucked them clean. He told her he wanted more.

"I'm all yours." He nodded and dropped before her. *"Are you going to eat me? Are you going to make me come here out in the open?"*

"Yes. Then I'm going to bite you. Here and here." He ran his fingers along her thigh and then up over her breast. *"Then I'm going to take you to the ground and, like a good bitch, you're going to roll to your knees and let me fuck you from behind. When I'm coming deep inside of you, I'm going to bite you again and again."*

He ran his tongue along the top of her panties, then tore them off her. Her scent hit his nose like she'd sprayed him with it. Licking her apex, he slid his hand up between her legs and slid his fingers into her heat. She was as wet as she was hot.

"You're so ready for me. Do you have any idea how delicious you taste? How much I enjoy having you come in my mouth over and over?" She moaned his name, and he cupped her ass and brought her closer to his mouth. Pressing his tongue past her wet curls and then past her lips, he suckled her clit into his mouth and nipped her.

She came hard, filling his mouth with hot juices that he swallowed down. Every time she trembled, every time she rolled her hips for more, he felt his beast, not the cat, but the one that really wanted her, snarl to be released. Brock fisted his cock and told her to get to her knees.

Her ass was presented to him where he wanted it. Her pussy still dripped with her need, and he could smell it. When he moved his cock near her entrance, she rolled back to him and he entered her with a hard punch of his hips. She cried out, and his beast roared.

"He wants to taste you." His voice sounded foreign to him, harsh and hard. *"I'm barely holding him back from biting you. I'm sorry, love. But I can't do this right now."* He started to pull from her body, but she reached between her legs and cupped his balls.

"Do it, Brock. Let him take me." The beast roared out his approval and told him she was his. *"Give me to him. Now, Brock, let him bite me and make me all of yours."*

His canines dropped so quickly that he hurt. But even as he told her he loved her, the beast yanked her back by her hair and bit her deep in the shoulder. Her screams in his head made him cry out for her, and the beast roared again that she was his as he filled her with his seed.

Brock lifted his head from her bloodied shoulder and threw back his head. She was theirs, all of theirs. He pulled from her then and snarled at her when she cringed from him. Rolling her to her back, he plunged into her, his cock pounding in her so hard that she moved along the dirt and gravel as he fell atop her. This time when he bit her he felt bone break and her flesh tear. Calming his beast was not possible, and he let him take her.

Even as he came again, he felt her tighten around him, her body milking his. Brock could feel her body begin the process of the change, and he was both excited and afraid. He lifted her up over him and held her to him as he leaned back on his knees. She was wrapping around him, tightening her grip on his body as she was his cock. When she ran her tongue along his shoulder, he knew she was going to bite him and begged her to do so. As soon as she drew blood, he came again, his saliva pouring into her opened wound. Falling to the ground, rolling so that he took both their weights, he held her to him.

Christ, he had no idea what had just happened, but he felt that whatever he'd been, that was what Em was going to be when her change was complete. Holding her to him, he looked up at the stars and felt both the beast and his cat rub along his skin. Brock reached for the beast, and when he snarled, he did it back. Closing his eyes, he saw him then.

"*You're mine as well.*" He nodded at Brock. "*I need you to obey me. You'll get us killed, and maybe our mate, too, if you take me like this again.*"

"*Danger. She is in danger.*" He told him he knew. "*We will protect what is ours. We will keep her safe.*"

Satisfied that nothing had been accomplished, Brock laughed to himself. The beast was right, she was in danger and they had to protect her. Rolling her to her back, he stood up and pulled on his jeans as he watched over her. Tomorrow he was going to take her out here again and show her how to shift. Picking her up, he wondered if she would even need his help. From what he'd seen so far, she could do anything she set her mind to.

Putting her into his bed, he covered her up and went to the bathroom. The beast shimmered along his face, as did his cat. They seemed to like each other, and he watched them seemingly chase each other. Turning off the light, he crawled into bed with her, and she rolled over him.

"*I love you.*" He kissed her forehead as she snuggled closer. "*I felt them. All of you, I felt them when you bit me.*"

"*I know, love. Are you hurt?*" She told him no. "*Tomorrow you're going to be sore, so I want you to try and rest a bit. Then when I get home tomorrow night we'll play.*"

"*Yes. I'll hunt you and mate with you as a tigress. They want to claim you as well.*" She sighed heavily, and he felt her fall asleep.

He wasn't surprised at all to hear her say there was more than one of her. He had thought she would have to in order to be his mate. As he drifted off to sleep, he felt the beast roll over his skin again, and he felt the comfort from him. Smiling, Brock let sleep take him.

~~~

Wilfred waited for over an hour for the humans to return. He thought about going into their home, but the one other time he'd been inside it he had vowed never to enter again. The place was a sty.

Dishes piled up on every flat surface in the house. Not just the kitchen, which, as far as Wilfred could see, had never seen either soap or water in months, maybe even decades. He had started to sit in one of the chairs but had heard the one that Harvey Owens had sat in creak loudly. Knowing he was bigger than the human, he stood because he didn't want to chance falling on his ass. And if he laughed, which he was sure he would, he'd have to kill him, but right now he needed him alive. He glanced around the neighborhood and wondered if anyone around here ever came out at night.

He saw movement just down the street and watched a woman walking her dog coming toward him. He started to take a step toward her when he saw a police cruiser flash his lights. The woman leaned into the car, and he heard the driver of the car tell her that she needed to get inside, that it wasn't safe out this late. As she hurried back in the direction she'd come, he watched the cruiser drive alongside her.

Had he wanted to, he could have snatched the woman from the sidewalk and had her drained before the cop ever knew what happened. But he could smell someone else coming his way, and he pulled the darkness around him. The large man startled him.

"You've no business here." He looked right at him, and Wilfred knew that he could see him despite the darkness that held him from others, human's, eyes. "I said you have no business here. The people who live here are no longer going to serve you, because I have taken care of them."

"Who are you and what the fuck do you mean you've taken care of them? They were mine." The man laughed, and it sent a chill down Wilfred's spine. Since becoming a vampire, Wilfred hadn't been afraid of anything or anyone, but this man, this vampire, frightened him just a little.

"I am Baron Wentcroft, master here, and much older than you by many millennium. You have no rights here unless I allow you to. You'll heed my words or suffer the consequences." Wilfred believed him, but he wasn't going to let him know that. "You think to defy me, child? I wouldn't if I were you. I'm much more than you can handle." Wilfred pretended indifference when all he wanted to do was bow before this man and offer him his throat.

"What of it? You say that you're this great and powerful lord? All I see is a man who hides in darkness and is no better than me. Maybe you should heed me when I tell you that I can do things that you've never dreamed of." He was baiting him, he knew, but he'd learned long ago that bravado was a much better tool than simply using his fists.

The man laughed. Wilfred wanted to hurt the man but knew that he wouldn't come out the winner on this round. And something that Wilfred prided himself on was always coming out on the winning side. He laughed, too, but even to his ears it sounded forced.

"You will leave this area tonight and forget you ever heard of us, much less have a sister. She is no longer yours to touch. She belongs to another, as you are well aware." Wilfred felt another shiver of fear and glared at the man, who only nodded. "Yes, I know a great deal about you. Your...brother...is very enlightening. You'd be amazed at how much he can give up when he thinks that he is only talking to a friend."

"Which brother did you speak to? Tell me his name, or so help me...." He would kill him. Whoever it was might as well meet the sun, because when Wilfred was through with him, he was going to wish for it. The man only tisked at him, shaking his head.

Just like his mother had done when he was a kid and she'd been disappointed in whatever he'd done. She was disappointed in him most of the time, now that he thought of it. Wilfred wondered what she'd think now if she could see the vampire he'd grown to be. Then he remembered that she, too, had tried to kill him. Mother and daughter were so much alike.

"She is well, you know?" Wilfred asked him who. "Your mother. The care that is being given her now has her on the road to recovery, and she will soon be a member of society again. She will still be troubled with nightmares, but she will regain what you took from her, you and the others."

"Took from her? We took nothing from her, but she tried to...you think I care about that bitch? She nearly got us all killed with her stories to the press and the neighbors. She wasn't supposed to tell anyone, and what does she do? She runs out and tells every fucking person who would stop to talk to her. And that fucking bitch Emma, you think I'm just going to walk away from her? Think again. She's a good as—"

His voice was cut off when the man was suddenly close enough that he could see his eyes. The deep blood-red color was a sign the vampire had been pushed too far and he was pissed. He knew that from the one and only time Jimmy had gotten that pissed at their mom and had ordered her killed. Wilfred felt himself being lifted off the ground, and even though he tried to kick out, nothing seemed to work. He hung there, trying to get free, as the man laughed again.

"You'll go home now or I'll make sure you and your entire male family regrets ever leaving your home and coming this far. Consider this your one and only warning, Wilfred Cole. The only one that will save your life. The next time we meet I will not go so easily on you." Wilfred was slammed against the house. He felt the impact throughout his entire body. As the man came toward him again, Wilfred felt his bladder let go. The man was the biggest vampire he'd ever seen. He made Jimmy look like a little kid. As he grew closer to Wilfred, he could feel his power nearly drip from him. He felt his own fear; fear for his life, and he hated that feeling.

"Mark my words, young Wilfred, you'll not feed on any human here so long as you stay on the path you are on. Your family will not feed so long as you disobey me and not return home as I have commanded you to." He was picked up again, and the man looked down at his wet pants. "You think that I'm frightening now, little boy? Wait until I come back for you. You'll wish for your mother's breast to comfort you and the darkness to hide you, but nothing will keep me from you. I will tear you apart as surely as you did all those people in that house."

Wilfred was dropped again, this time into a pile of shit that he'd avoided all evening waiting for the Owens to return. He didn't move but stayed where he was as the vampire moved out of the yard and faded into the night. He was ready to stand up and go back to his lair when the vampire turned again. All Wilfred could see was his face.

"You have two days. At the end of those two days, I will find you." He was fading away when Wilfred felt the touch of his mind. *"When I return, Wilfred Robin Cole, I will not be as easy on you as you were on your last victims. Death will not comfort you in the afterlife, for I will bring you back many times to kill you over and over until I tire of it."*

Wilfred didn't move. He'd known about his last meal? Not possible. Standing up, he entered the house behind him and searched for something to put on. All he could find was a pair of worn jeans that were too short for his legs and hung low on his hips. The shirt, probably the only clean one in the house, had been hanging in the bathroom on a hanger, still damp.

Wilfred took a quick shower and put on the clothes and wondered again where the family was. They had seemed so eager to do work for him, and he'd been thinking about giving himself another child or two. The ones that he'd made so far had spread out to do their own thing, and he hadn't heard from them other than once when one of them died. Not a great loss to him, as he'd fathered three, but he still felt the pang of it.

Wilfred thought about what the man had said and dismissed him. He had done nothing but yap, and now that he'd thought about it, had done nothing but brag about this unseen greatness. No power poured from Baron whatever as it had Jimmy until the end right before he'd left him. Jimmy had assured them all that they would know power when it approached them. Wilfred had felt nothing but fear, and that was more than likely all the power that he had, the gift of fear. But one of his brothers had talked.

He was trying to figure out which one as he entered the lair. The sun would be coming up soon, and he felt the drag of it on his body. That was the one thing he hated more than anything, the sun's pull on him. It shorted his night and made him so weak during its time that he cursed it. Wilfred was sitting in the room's only chair when his dad and brothers came in.

He hated his dad. He was nothing more than an old man who tried to tell him what to do. Wilfred was nearly thirty years old, well past him being ordered around by his father, especially one as weak as he was. He glared at him as the other three talked about their night. He thought about telling them he hoped they fed well because this was the last night for them, but he didn't believe that any more than he did anything else the Baron had told him. But he did watch them.

One of them had had to talk to the other vampire. But which one? All of them knew his full name, as he did theirs. All of them also knew that he had a temper as well, so the last victim shit was just that, bullshit. He watched Steven. He would have the most to gain if the vampire would be able to kill him, but Wilfred didn't see that happening. Next to him he was the strongest. He never considered his dad because the Baron had said brother.

Maybe he should try bluffing. He'd always been good at it before he'd changed, and he felt now that he was so powerful that he'd be an expert at it. He'd actually thought of going to one of those all-night games and winning at poker, but he didn't care all that much for money, as he had as much as he wanted from stealing from the homes he'd broken into. Sitting back, he watched them start to crawl around on the floor trying to find a place that would be comfortable during their rest. He'd taken the only bed to the basement just last night and had been sleeping on it. There was no way he was laying on the floor on the main level of the house so that anyone or anything could come in and bring the sun with them.

"I saw another vampire today." Nothing from any of them, so he continued. "He said that we were to leave this area and never to return. And that if we didn't, he'd hunt us down and kill us all. He also said my full name, like that was supposed to be scary or something." It had been, but he wasn't going to tell them that.

"Why?" This from Steven. "What business is it of his where we are? Do you think that Emma sent him? Or did you tell him where we are just to be bragging again?"

Wilfred sat up. "Why would she send anyone for us? She doesn't know we're coming, does she? I mean, someone would have had to say something to someone for him to know that we're in town. He also knew about the party we had the other night. And my name? How do you suppose he was able to get my full name?" Not all true, but how the fuck would they know unless they told him the truer parts.

Steven shrugged. As he lay down on the blanket and settled in, Wilfred was ready to try Shawn when his brother spoke again. "Maybe she knows him. Maybe she has told him all sorts of things about us. She never was one to talk much, but we know that vampires can read minds. Hell, for all we know, she could be his mate that Dad was talking about. We should probably think about what he wants us to do. I'm not all that keen about being killed right now."

Anger surged over him, and Wilfred tried to control it. If he tried to kill him now, with the others so close, he might get hurt. He watched as death took them, fighting his own rest. As soon as they were all no longer breathing, he went to the fireplace, picked up a piece of kindling, and broke it in two so that he had a sharp point at the end. Standing over his brother, he felt his fangs drop in anticipation of staking him. He knelt down beside him and kissed his brother's forehead.

"You should never fuck with anyone stronger than you, brother dear." He plunged the wood deep into his chest, feeling the moment that it pierced his heart. His brother woke as blood poured from his chest, mouth, and ears. Black and vile smelling, it spilled to the floor, and curls of smoke came up from it. His fangs dropped, and he hissed at him as he tried to pull the wood from his heart. Holding it where it was, deep in his brother's chest, Wilfred smiled at his brother as he began to burn. His brother would be no more in a matter of seconds.

Standing up, he watched as his body incinerated and dust covered the floor. Looking at his other two brothers, he was tempted to do the same to them and his dad. But he might need them. Looking at his dad again, he smiled. He was next. He even thought about doing it now, but the sun was heating the room, and he needed his rest.

Staggering to the basement, he looked around. He couldn't just lay out where they could find him if they wanted, and crawled up the stairs again to the attic. He barely got the door closed when he pitched forward. Christ, he was going to hurt himself as he fell and knew it. But he was out before he touched the first rat droppings that covered the entire floor. He needed a safer resting place.

~~~

Peter woke with a start and smiled. He had felt the moment that one of his…grandchildren, he supposed…had died. One down and four to go until he rid the world of their evilness. He felt another…disturbance in the line, and realized that Em had felt the death too. He thought that odd, but she was their sister and maybe it was true that families could feel when a member was killed violently. But as he lay back, he felt Brock as well when he stirred awake. Getting up from his resting place, he went to the window and reached for his maker.

"*One has killed the one of their kind tonight. There are now only four of them left, sire.*" He waited for a response, and when none was forthcoming, he spoke again. "*There was…I think that Emma felt the passing. Could it be that she is connected to them still?*"

"*No. I think…the male, her mate, he also felt it. They are very strong, are they not, Peter? They are not like the other cats in the streak.*" Peter told him he didn't think so and told him about the strange thing that had happened with Brock that day. "*Hmm. Do you think he is more than a mere cat? Do you think that what we had hoped is now coming true?*"

He didn't know. "*I believe him to be much more than a simple shifter, and if the other is true then he will be something…more than likely more than either of us dreamed he could. He has an aggressiveness about him that I've never encountered before. And as his mate, and now I think his true mate, she is surer of herself as well.*"

"It bears watching...the two of them, I mean. I don't mean to say they'll cause trouble, but the simple fact that they are so different will make it so we keep an eye on them. We have many plans for this family, and all of them will need to be together before this is completed. All of them." Viktor laughed. "The female, Emma, has she come to be friendlier with you?"

"Yes. She is still slightly standoffish, but she is coming around. The day she sipped from me made me think her to be coming around, but it's hard to tell." He lay back down on his bed. "You'll be coming for a visit then? You'll be here when my children come to see them?"

"I will. I do not think they cannot win against him, especially since they have begun to kill each other off. The one called Wilfred, he is mad with his newfound power and will be stupid with it. He might just kill himself before they get to your family."

He hoped so, but Peter didn't hold out much hope. In his experience, people like Wilfred would go along for a long time being the way he was, mean and without any kind of repercussions laid at his door, before someone would come along and have to kill him. He knew that Wilfred would kill his father and possibly another brother, but that would just make him feel as if he could win against higher odds. He would have to be killed before much longer. He hoped that he would be there when it happened, too.

Chapter 9

Brock rolled over in the bed and found a cold place where he thought Em should have been. He listened to see if she'd gone to the bathroom, but there didn't seem to be any sound coming from there either. Rising, he reached for her and found her in the kitchen with his cook. He smiled as he got into the shower.

"Are you sore still?" She was embarrassed, and he nearly laughed. *"I meant your shoulder, love. I know that my beast broke your bones when he bit you."*

"I'm okay. I'd forgotten about it until you just mentioned it." She paused, and he felt her fear, but before he could comment on it, she continued. *"I think my family is nearer. Last night...Brock, I think one of them is dead."*

He'd felt something, too, but had thought it was just a dream and had simply gone back to sleep. He was curious as to why he might have felt the death of a vampire, but there wasn't much about his life right this minute that he understood. He would ask Peter. He was his only source in this matter. He got into the shower as he spoke to her.

"I think you're right. I don't know why I think so, but I'm pretty sure I felt it too. We need to talk to Peter as soon as we can. He might know the reason you felt it, or even if that's what we felt. It might just be a bad dream." Or hopeful thinking too, maybe on both their parts. *"I'll be down soon. I love you."*

"I love you as well. And your mom is here. She said she needs to speak to you." He sighed, knowing she wanted something he wasn't going to be able to give her. *"She said you'd better not try and duck her again or she'll have your hide. Sheesh, your mom is intense."*

"You have no idea." Brock finished up his shower and dressed in some tear away pants and a tee-shirt. He was going to go with Em today and help her shift. He'd wanted to last night, but they'd both been so exhausted that he wasn't sure that if there was an emergency he could have helped anyone. Smiling, he thought it was the best reason in the world to call in sick.

His mom was sitting at the table, frowning. He didn't see Em anywhere but wasn't worried because no one else seemed to be. When he sat down, a plate of food was placed in front of him by Roland, and he offered some to his mom.

"No. You know as well as I do that I was at a breakfast meeting you were supposed to be at with me. You figured sleeping in was a good excuse not to go with me? I'll have you know that I was embarrassed since you were supposed to introduce me as a guest speaker." He sat back, embarrassed himself. He should have been there.

"I converted Em last night, and I completely forgot." She looked at him oddly, then at Em when she entered the room. "We got back here and it just happened. I know I'm supposed to—"

He stopped talking when his mom stood up. She leaned into Em, who took a step back, and then looked at him. He couldn't read the look on her face. It was sort of a cross between her being upset and confused.

"I don't smell you on her. I mean not at all. It's as if you've never touched her." He looked at Roland, who shrugged. "Brock, I don't even smell her on you as her mate at all, and I should. We all should."

Brock stood up and buried his nose in Em's throat. She wrapped her hands around his arms and held him as he pulled her to him. Their cats seemed to touch, and he lifted his head to look at his mom. She looked shocked.

"That I felt. Good heavens, son, what did you do to her? I felt…I think I felt her cat rub her head on my throat. I've never felt that…never in all my years have I felt anything like that. It was as if she marked me." He reached for her, and she backed up. "Not yet. I think I need to have a seat."

Roland shoved a chair under her, and his mom sat down and stared at Em. Em didn't flinch or fidget like he was known to do when his mom looked at him like that. In fact all of them did, even big bad-assed Ryland. He sat down, too, and pulled Em into his lap to wait.

"She's an enforcer like you." Before he could ask his mom what she meant, she took Em's hand. "I've never known a female enforcer, though I don't doubt they exist. You're his true other half, his mate in all ways. My goodness, dear, you are going to be a thing to reckon with, aren't you, when the two of you are together?"

Em shook her head and looked at him. He didn't know what to say to her either. He didn't understand any of this, and he was pretty sure his mom didn't either. Em took out her pad of paper and started writing. He watched as she handed it to his mom.

"I don't know, dear. I honestly don't. When they get here, and we all know they are coming, I would bet that they'll have a hard time even getting close to you, much less trying to take you now. I'm pretty sure that you could kick their asses all by yourself, and I for one want to be there when you do. I'll be sure to bring my camera and some popcorn. I think it'll be entertaining to say the least." She sat back after handing him the note. "I think I might like to see the look on Ryland's face too when he finds out. He'll have...what was that saying I heard the other day...? Kitten? He'll have a kitten?" Em laughed with his mom.

"I'm thinking we need to talk to Peter, too." Both women nodded. "But about Ryland...I thought he felt when someone was converted because he was our male. You think he didn't feel hers?"

His mom smiled and shook her head. "I saw him this morning at the breakfast, and he didn't mention it, and I'm sure he would have. By the way, he's not happy with you either since I gave him an earful. Now that I know why...I'm so happy for you both. I'm sure that he'll not be too happy with you when he gets here."

Brock wasn't sure, but he had a feeling his brother was going to be really pissed off. Not just because he'd not asked for permission, but because he'd embarrassed their mom. Ryland, as all the boys, loved their mom. They were afraid of her, too, but they loved her. He smiled when he heard someone pull into his driveway and lifted Em off his lap to go out and greet his brother. There was no sense in messing up the kitchen for this. Brock had a feeling his brother was going to hit first and ask questions later.

As soon as Ryland got out of the car and came around it, he found himself on the ground. His fist had shot out so quickly that Brock had had no time to react. Before he could get up and tell him he was sorry, he heard a crash and saw a blur of gold and black streak past him.

Ryland was pinned against the car hood with a tiger at his throat. She held him there with the weight of her body, and Ryland didn't, or maybe couldn't, move. Brock was still trying to wrap his mind around where she had come from when his mom touched his arm. He looked at her.

"Do something before she kills him." He looked at the cat and realized it was Em. "She just shifted and was crashing out the door before I could blink. I've never seen anyone shift like that before. Nearly had me wet my drawers."

He wasn't going to comment on that and slowly made his way to the car. He whispered through her mind and was surprised to find his cat wanting to kill Ryland as well. Brock's cat and the beast moved along his skin, and Em growled.

"He didn't hurt me. Please back off before he shifts and hurts you, love. Em, can you hear me? Let Ryland go." He ran his hand down her back over her fur, trying his best to get through to her before one of them got hurt. *"Christ, do you have any idea how beautiful you are right now? You're much bigger than I thought you'd be as a cat, and much meaner. Ryland is going to be pissed when you let him go."*

"He hit you." He heard her voice and was surprised at the hatred that came from her. *"He will not hurt what's mine."*

Brock was trying really hard not to be too proud of her and looked at Ryland. He was pissed, he could see that, but he thought he saw he was impressed, too. He spoke to Ryland as he rubbed Em's fur.

"I converted her last night." Ryland spoke to him through their link and told him "no shit." "She's not happy because you hit me. I'm trying to calm her, but if you let me tell her that you won't punish her too badly, I think I can get her to let you go."

"I have no intentions of punishing her at all so long as she fucking lets me go. I should have…I didn't know you'd done this. Why didn't you fucking tell somebody?" Brock shrugged.

"Please have your mate let go of my throat before she brings my mate to me."

His voice was so calm that Brock laughed. He'd sounded like he was requesting that Brock go to the movies with him or something. Brock leaned his face into Em's throat. He got a mouth full of fur, but he bit her.

"Let him go." She growled again but lifted her head from Ryland. *"Now get back so he can stand. You've been a bad girl, and I will spank you if you don't do as I say."*

Her cat purred at him, but she looked back at Ryland and growled again. He watched as they made eye contact, and could feel the connection like the one between he and Ryland snap into place. He heard Ryland swear, but just then Em leapt off him and sat next to their mom. Brock wasn't sure, but if either of them took a step toward their mom, Em wouldn't hesitate in ripping their throats out, and damn the law that said that she couldn't hurt her mate.

Ryland sat up and leaned against the car. He had blood on his neck where she'd bitten him, and Brock realized that was how they had connected. He started for Ryland to see how bad it was when Em growled. They looked where she was when she suddenly took off to the house. A car was coming up the driveway.

"Who is it?" Brock shrugged at his mom. "She must know who it is. She took off like she was afraid."

"It's to do with my family. I'll wait in here. And if you need me, I'll come out. I don't know what he wants, but he smells like them." Brock told his mom and brother who Em thought he was, and that she was waiting to see if they needed her. Ryland looked at him as the car came to a stop. He wasn't any happier now than before, but at least he wasn't hitting him again.

"She's going to have to explain to me what the fuck happened here. And she's going to have to pledge to Bronwyn too." He looked back at the house for a second before watching with him the little man who got out of the car. "Christ, do you have any idea how much power she has? She could have killed me and there wouldn't have been a damned thing I could have done about it. And I'm pretty fucking sure she would have had you not commanded her to release me."

He only had a chance to nod before the little man was standing in front of them. He was human, and he did smell of vampires. He smiled nervously as he wiped sweat from his face and neck and held out his hand. Neither of them took it.

"I'm here on behalf of the family of Emma Cole." He put his hand down and frowned. "My name is Saul McKinney, and I would like to speak to Miss—"

"So?" The man looked at Ryland, then back at him as he continued. "Say what you have to say and get the hell off my property. You have no rights here, and, frankly, you're very close to having me call the police."

"I have some information on Miss Cole that you need to be made aware of. Her family is requesting that you cooperate so that this can be settled amicably. She needs to be brought home so that she can be treated." The man looked over his shoulder, and Brock knew that Em had come out of the house. But when he turned, he saw his mom coming toward them.

"You'll tell us what she's being treated for, young man, or so help me, whatever they think of doing to you, I'm going to be much worse. Spill it." He and Ryland both took a step back to get out of her way. "Well? Do you think we have all day? Say whatever is burning a hole in your throat before I hurt you. I've had a really crappy morning so far, and you being here is not making it any better. I just might have to hurt you so that something feels right."

"She's nuts." The man flushed when their mom took a step toward him. "What I mean to say is that Miss Cole is ill. Her mother suffers from the same illness. They believe that the males in the family are vampires. And until recently Miss Cole was being treated by a doctor who was working on getting her to where she was well enough to be on a release program."

"He is lying. I'm betting he doesn't believe in weretigers either. Maybe if I came out there and pissed all over his nice suit, then changed to me, he'd believe fast enough." Brock covered his mouth and smiled. He told Em to behave and to stay inside but to remain a cat.

"We'll use your plan later if necessary. Maybe not the shifting part, but the pissing on him part. Hell, I think my mom might join you." He looked at the man and spoke to him. "You say she was being treated? Where? And for how long?"

"Where?" The man reached into the inside of his coat and froze when a loud growl came from Brock's mom. "I think...I believe that I should simply go back to the Cole family and express a desire to quit their services."

He moved so quickly to his car that he dropped the papers out of the file. Ryland had just picked them all up when McKinney turned to them. He looked ready to bolt, but he came back and handed Brock another file. He didn't explain but got into his car and left. Brock turned to his family.

"He'll not be back." His mom laughed. "And you scared him when you growled. What was that all about?"

"I thought he was reaching for a gun. It's that show I was watching last night. Some gangster show that had me up half the night watching it and the other half worrying that someone was gunning for me. That charming man in that show looked like he was as sweet as honey, but he had such a dark side too." She shivered. "Well, it got rid of him quick enough, didn't it? So I would appreciate it if you'd back the hell up off me, thank you very much."

She huffed at him and turned on her heel and moved toward his house. When she disappeared behind the broken door that he just noticed, Brock looked at Ryland. He looked pole axed.

"I'm going to have to put a rating on her television. She's getting more and more like Bronwyn every day. I think maybe the two of them need to stop hanging out together, too. She's become really scary lately." Brock threw back his head and laughed at his brother. "You try having her watch your kid one of these days. Just last night I caught her reading Gabby *Crime and Punishment*. And she was reading it in a voice that sounded like she was reading her a fairytale story. Scared the shit out of me."

Brock took his brother in the house. When he asked where Em was, Roland said she'd left him in the kitchen not a minute ago. He assumed she'd gone up to change. Brock nodded and handed his brother a bottle of beer. It was only ten in the morning, but he drank it down like it was his last meal. He sat the empty bottle on the table and looked at his mom, then at him.

"What the fuck happened here today?"

~~~

Em went down to the kitchen after shifting back. It hadn't hurt her either time, but she could feel the pull of a couple of muscles. She looked at Brock, then at Ryland. He was probably going to yell at her. She handed him the note she'd written before coming down.

"I'm sorry. I don't know what came over me, but when I saw you hit Brock, I needed to kill you. I didn't mean to hurt you, and I'll pay whatever fine there is that you feel I owe you." He handed it back to her.

"You should know that I would have done the same thing." She didn't understand what he meant and tried to hand him the note again. "I know you're sorry. And it's mostly my fault. I should have asked him what happened before I went off half-cocked and hit him. I wasn't aware that he'd changed you."

Taking out her pad, he touched it and she looked at him. There was that feeling that she was a part of him again, and her cat stirred under her skin. Em hadn't told Brock yet, but she felt like there were two of them in her and they both had wanted to kill this man.

"You can speak to me now. When you took my blood and we made the connection, we can now speak to each other. I know you can with Bronwyn, but I think you still need to pledge to her." Em nodded. *"Good. Now, I'd like to talk to you about the man who said that —"*

Brock handed him a file, and Em looked at him. *"There's a bunch of pictures of you and me together in town. I think someone has been following us for about a week now if I'm seeing that right. And also there's a committal paper in there that is dated about two weeks ago. It basically says that you're under a doctor's care and that you need to be kept under lock and key. Your father signed it."*

"He put my mom away a long time ago. He said she was insane to think that they were all vampires." Brock nodded. *"You don't believe that, do you? I know you are aware there really are vampires, but I mean that my mom is insane. Well, she might be a little, but not about what she was saying."*

"No. I know there are vampires as well as other creatures. But we need to contact someone to find out what's going on." Sandra sat down next to her at the table and smiled. "Something isn't right here, and I don't mean just with your family coming. You were going to kill Ryland and shifted like someone who had done it before. Mom said you startled her when you did."

"I've contacted Alistair. He can get this straightened out. He's coming here now to get these papers. He said that Peter is with him. He was bringing him here so that he could speak to you both." Sandra patted her hand as she continued. "I think that there is more going on here than these ridiculous papers. I think that that man was to lure you away so that they could get you. I can't believe I didn't think of that before and rip his throat out for good measure. I guess you can't really kill the messenger though. But I do believe that you're much more than a simple tiger, and I think we all know it."

Em was afraid of that too. She looked at Brock, who winked at her. She flushed when she realized that Ryland had seen him do that. The man was so much bigger than her, yet she'd tried to kill him not half an hour ago.

When Peter and Alistair showed up, she was ready to run. Peter made her uncomfortable still, but not like before. She didn't think he'd harm her, but he still made her feel like he was about to do something to her. She watched as he stood near the door and didn't speak. She watched as Alistair went over the papers that had been out of the file as well as the ones that had been in the one that Brock had. She looked up when she felt someone touch her mind. It was Peter.

"You and I are related, though I'm not sure how." She looked at Brock, then at Peter. "You felt the moment your brother was killed, as did I. Do you know which one is dead?"

"*Steven. He's the oldest. I think Wilfred killed him.*" Peter nodded. "*Why can I feel them when they die, and how do I know who did it? Also, you said we're related; how is that even possible? I've never seen you before moving here.*"

He didn't move, and she was aware that no one else seemed to know they were talking and looked at Brock again. He and Ryland, along with Alistair and their mom, were looking over some of the papers. Peter smiled when she looked at him.

"*The man Jimmy, the one that turned your family, he was my child. When he was killed not long ago, his children became a responsibility to me. Is he the one who gave you that scar, too?*" She nodded. "*I thought so. He was trying to convert you as well, and I'm assuming that's when the connection was formed.*" He moved to the chair on the other side of her and held out his hand. "*My maker is concerned that they will harm you, but...you're not human any longer, are you?*"

"*No. We did the conversion thing last night.*" Peter nodded. "*But something else happened. I don't think it worked like it was supposed to. I can feel something else. I think it's another cat inside of me.*"

"*It's the match to Brock's. He calls him his beast, and I'm reasonably sure that he is. He comes out when he needs him most. Like the other day when we were all together and you'd been hurt.*" She looked at the others before Peter continued. "*You're a rare and wonderful creature, Emma. And as such you'll not be harmed by your family ever again. But I need your help, that of you and Brock. They need to be destroyed. Your brothers have killed a great many people, and they need to be rid from this place.*"

She thought about her brothers and father. They were horrible beings even when they'd been humans...cruel to people who did nothing to them, stealing from others when there was no reason to. Nothing or no one had been safe from their cruelty, and now that they were vampires, she was pretty sure that they didn't improve with the change. She looked at Peter and nodded.

"*Tell me what you need me to do. But Wilfred is mine. He's the one that held me down when Jimmy bit me. I have some payback to give him.*" Peter nodded.

Chapter 10

Bert looked around again. There was no sign of Steven anywhere. And he couldn't find Wilfred either. He was just about ready to go out and look for them both, something making him think that they'd been hurt, but he nearly fell over in relief when Wilfred came from the attic. He looked behind him to see if his brother was with him, but he wasn't there.

"He's gone off on his own." Bert looked at Wilfred when he volunteered the information. "Last night after you all went to rest, he said he'd had enough and was going back home. He said to tell you he'd see you there when you got back."

"Home? Why? I thought he was going to help us bring your sister home. We all agreed to change her here and take her back before her first rising." Wilfred shrugged, and for some reason Bert didn't believe him. "What really happened to your brother? Did the two of you get into a fight?"

He'd started to add "again" on the end of that statement but didn't. There was enough tension in the air that you could choke on it. When Wilfred stretched his neck muscles, Bert had a feeling that Wilfred was trying his best not to attack him, and that made Bert take a few steps back. Then he looked at where his son had been sleeping last night.

There was a faint outline where he'd been, like the floor surrounding him had been scorched. He nearly leaned over and looked at it but stopped at the last second. Wilfred was looking at him again with a look that said "go ahead and do it." Fear curled around his belly, and he took a step back.

"You all should get a good meal in your bellies. As soon as it's dark enough, we're going to pay our little solicitor a call and see if he got to talk to the Goldens." Shawn and Erwin looked to him, and he nodded. He felt anger boil off Wilfred and looked at him.

"Soon they'll be looking to me for answers and not you, old man. You're nothing but an incompetent fool, and we all know it." Bert was surprised by the venom in his son's voice. "You'll see. I should have been made in charge from the very beginning, and there would be no way that Emma would have gotten this far."

"She's near here, and we'll get her back. She will learn her place, and when she does, we can go back to being a family again." Wilfred grinned, and the hair on Bert's arms danced. "You should go and feed."

Wilfred nodded, and when he left, Bert sat down on the floor and took several deep breaths. His son had scared him, and not just a little, either. Looking at the place on the floor, Bert ran his fingers over the area, and his fingertips came away with soot on them. He leaned down to sniff the area and jumped back. It was Steven. Someone had killed him. And Bert knew it had been Wilfred.

But why? What would have driven him to murder his own brother, not to mention doing it right before they were so close to getting all that they'd come for? He tried to remember the conversation last night, and only remembered that Wilfred had been upset about talking to a vampire, and he'd known his full name. But why that would be enough to cause him to murder him, he didn't know.

By the time the others had returned, Bert was no closer to figuring how what to do about Wilfred than he'd been before. He'd gone out to get a quick meal, not able to get his fill from the woman he'd pulled into the darkness. He'd been able to bite her, but not feed. She was dead by now anyway, as he'd neither bothered closing the wounds at her throat, nor worked very hard at concealing her body. What the hell was going on? He had a dead son that he was sure his brother had killed, a daughter to bring back, and now he couldn't feed. He wondered if Wilfred had anything to do with that, too.

They went to McKinney's office and found the place locked up tight and all the lights off.

"He said he'd meet us here after the sun went down." Shawn looked in the windows and then around the yard. "His car isn't even here. Where the fuck could he be?"

"He's probably at home watching television with his family. The mother fucker is going to pay for this." Wilfred broke the window and nearly tore the door off the hinges, opening it up. "We'll just wait for him here. If he's not here within the hour, we'll go and see if we can find him on our own."

The waiting only lasted until the first cruiser pulled into the lot less than five minutes later. When the second one pulled in almost immediately, they all went out the back door of the building and spread out like cockroaches when the light came on. Bert found himself teaming up with Erwin when they found a hidey hole by crawling into a hollowed-out log.

"They sure were fast." Bert nodded. "It's almost as if they knew we were in there. We probably set off one of them alarms and they sent the police after us."

"Wilfred didn't check when he just opened the door by breaking in. I would have checked first to see." Bert had no idea why he'd said that to his son, and knew that he wouldn't have checked for an alarm either. "He's going to get us caught. And what will happen if we're in a jail cell when the sun comes up?"

Erwin looked at him like he'd never thought of that. In fact, Bert hadn't thought of it either until that very second.

They'd been moving along all this time as if they were omnipotent, and they were more fragile now than they'd been as humans. At least as a human they'd been a great deal more cautious when they'd been bullies. Now they had become stupid, lazy even. He wondered how much they'd left of them behind when they'd killed the other night at that party and shivered. Fuck, they'd been stupid. But not anymore. At least he wasn't planning on it from now on. He thought for a moment and decided that having his daughter home with them wasn't a good idea, and wanted to go back home. There they were safe.

He turned to tell Erwin about his thoughts on it when he saw someone approaching them. They both hunkered down behind the log that they'd been hiding in when a voice, a strong and cultured voice, reached them.

"You're going about this all wrong. When you break and enter into a lawyer's home, you should always expect a security system in place." Bert looked at Erwin, who had fallen asleep. He reached to wake him when the voice spoke again. "Leave him be. Your other son, Wilfred, is trying to get you killed. Are you aware of that?"

"Who are you?" All he got in answer was laughter, cold and chilling laughter. "Show yourself to me now or I'll come out after you."

"No you won't. You're not only too afraid of your own shadow, but you're also mine and you cannot harm me." The laughter again, and it made his skin crawl. "You've no opinion on your son? Did he tell you that you can no longer feed? That because of him I've taken that away from you? You know that he killed the oldest, Steven, don't you? Why haven't you confronted him? Found out the answers that burn in your mind?"

Because, as the man said, he was afraid, but he wouldn't say that to anyone, especially to one he didn't know. He looked at Erwin and wondered if the man out there had done something to him, and when he woke, it would be too late to get indoors. He shivered, thinking about what Jimmy had told them about what happened when they were caught in the sun.

"You should heed his words. Jimmy would know more than others what happens when the sun touches our bodies. Though I must tell you, he cannot tell you himself now. Because of his crimes, he is no longer substance, but ash in the wind." That terrified Bert a great deal, and he wasn't even sure why. "Of course you know why. You think that your son is going to leave you out in it. He might, too. He is unlike any of you. He has no qualms about killing his own kind."

"You lie." The heat seared his skin almost as soon as the words left his mouth, and he fell back from it. He looked up to see a man, large and dark, as he hovered just above him in the starless night. Bert tried to scramble away from him but only succeeded in getting lodged against the log tighter. Terror rolled over him, and he whimpered like a child, more like a dog.

"I do not lie." The man, a vampire he could tell, now faded out as he continued. "You will find out soon enough. The next one he tries to kill will be you. Should you find yourself...when he attacks, you simply say 'I command you to back off.' It may work. Then again it may not. We'll see, will we not?"

"I don't understand. Why is he going to kill me? I've done nothing to him. And I'm his father. He loves me." Bert knew that to be a lie the moment he said it. "He cannot kill his own kind. Jimmy told us that."

"Did he tell you that you *couldn't* or that you *shouldn't*?" Bert couldn't remember. There had been so many rules, and he'd not really been paying attention.

"He can kill us then. Kill all of us without anyone caring at all." He sounded afraid, even to his own ears. "What is the point of all this power if someone like us can kill us without anyone doing anything about it?"

"You mean like the people in the house that you killed? Or the ones you've murdered on the way here? Someone will pay for all those crimes, trust me. And as you are as guilty as your sons, you'll pay the price as well. The sun does not care who it touches when we stake you out in it," Erwin stirred as the man faded. "He comes now to tell you that you're the problem. I would be careful of him."

As soon as Wilfred came into view, Erwin sat up and looked at him, too. There was something very off about his second oldest son, and he was sure that the man was right. Wilfred was going to kill him.

"Where the fuck did you go?" His fist lashed out before either he or Erwin could move from it. "You were supposed to spread out and come back to see if the rest of us were caught. What the fuck did you suppose was going to happen if we were taken to jail?"

"You'd have had the sun touch you." Erwin didn't move fast enough after he spoke, and he was suddenly flying across the wooded area as soon as Wilfred touched him. When he hit the tree, Bert heard his bones break, and then suddenly Erwin was aflame. He must have hit a broken branch, and it entered him at his heart. Both he and others watched as Erwin burned out and his ash rained to the floor of the forest.

"Mother fuck." Shawn looked at them. "You killed him. You fucking killed him. You know what Jimmy said…there would be consequences if you killed one of our own."

"Fuck Jimmy. What the fuck good is it to quote him when he left us to fend for ourselves? And what the fuck was I supposed to do when he makes an idiotic statement like that? Agree with him? You said yourself that he and Dad should have come back for us when we were caught."

They'd been caught? He looked at his two sons very closely. They were covered in blood. Christ, they'd killed while he talked to the vampire. He stood up and looked at the tree where his baby had been killed, and then at Wilfred.

"Is it your plan to kill us all off before we can get Emma?" Wilfred didn't even try to deny it, but walked to where he and Erwin had been sitting and picked up the bag that Erwin had had on him when they'd left the house. "I asked you a question. Are you planning to kill us like you did Steven and Erwin?"

"I'll do whatever it takes. And whatever I have to do to bring her back. She's fucking going to do what I tell her, when I tell her, or she'll earn the same fate as those two." Bert looked at Shawn as Wilfred walked deeper into the woods.

"So you did kill Steven. And those others, did you kill those cops, too?" Shawn nodded when Wilfred didn't. "Did *you* kill them or did Wilfred? Because either way it went down, we're going to be in big trouble when someone finds out. We've not been taking precautions to keep anyone from finding us. And they will, too. And once they do, we're as good as dead."

"We're vampires. They can't hurt us." Bert pointed to the tree where his brother had just been killed. "That was Wilfred, not a stupid human. If we're going to just get Emma, then we should go and do it, then get back home and pretend none of this ever happened."

Bert followed Shawn in the direction that Wilfred had gone. He thought about what the other vampire had said. They were going to pay. Bert thought of all the things they'd done and figured that they were all going to be staked. If that was so, then it didn't matter if they killed or not. He smiled. They might as well have as much fun as they could before then. He reached out and put his hand on Shawn's shoulder.

"I need to feed; I couldn't earlier, could you?" Shawn shook his head. "You want to come with me and find a nice, big place for us to stay that has heat and running water? We could have a lot of fun if there are humans in the house." Shawn grinned.

"I'd like that. Wilfred said we were commanded not to feed, and he said it was entirely your fault. That we'd been cursed because you can't keep your mouth shut." Shawn didn't notice that he'd stopped walking as he continued. "I don't believe him, of course, but it is really strange that we can't get a meal now."

"I didn't do anything, Shawn. I swear to you. And I don't doubt that Wilfred is the reason we can't feed." Bert looked around as if Wilfred might be close enough to hear them.

"Why don't you and I find a meal and a place to flop until we get Emma? See if it's really true we can't feed. And we need to find out where these people live that McKinney was telling us about, too. Golden, didn't he say?"

"Yeah. He said something about Golden Towers. We should pay them a visit tomorrow night. I think it might be fun to scare the rich prick and feed on a building full of stupid humans." Bert agreed. The voice was going to have to find himself someone who cared what he had to say. Bert and his sons were going to make their mark.

~~~

Brock got up to pace. What Keith was telling him couldn't be true. He glanced over at Jules, who nodded. There was no way that he and Em both had real wild tigers as their beasts. He sat down, only to hop back up again.

"Sit down. For Christ's sake, I've never seen anyone move as much as you do." Bronwyn lifted her brow at him when he didn't sit. Honestly, he wasn't sure if he cared if she hurt him or not. He needed to—

"What makes you think that this thing I call my beast isn't just...I don't know, my own cat with more attitude?" He looked at his mom, who had been quiet since his family showed up an hour ago. Just as he and Em were about to go out into the woods and play. "You said yourself that you have nothing much to go on. What if what you're saying is an old tale that someone thought was funny?"

"Because we've all felt them stirring under your skins, and it comes from both of you." Ryland handed him the copied sheets that he said he'd taken from their old books. "Mom said she remembered something, and she said she told you the story about the cub. We think when he bit you, he gave you something else, something that made it so you'd be different than all the others who came before you."

Brock looked at Em, who was watching Bronwyn. She'd said she would make sure that Em understood them and what was going on. He didn't understand Ryland and was pretty sure she didn't either by the look on her face. She looked at him and smiled. He could tell she was afraid, but he wasn't sure how to comfort her. Not with his mind working overtime on the information they were putting before him.

"Enforcers can't find their mates. You did." Brock nodded at Ryland without turning to look at him. "You said yourself that you have no control over him. Or at the very least, very little control. It's because he's not like you. He's more."

"And because of this extra...whatever you called it, I'm something of a freak." His mom stood up, and before he could tell her he was sorry, she slapped him.

The beast roared, but he didn't try to come forth. Instead, his beast lowered his head when she looked him in the eye. He wanted to do the same, but she held his chin up.

"What does he want to do to me?" Brock tried to look away. "Tell me, Brock, what does he want to do to me for slapping you?"

"Nothing. Nothing at all. He's sort of like me when I disappoint you. Cowering and hoping you'll find someone else to yell at before I become a puddle in the floor." She nodded and smiled. "And you find this to be funny why?"

"Not funny, but what I thought. I raised the little cub up, and he knows that. He would never harm me. I doubt very much that hers would either." They both turned to Em, who shook her head.

"She was upset, but she didn't make me feel murderous like when Ryland hit you." She looked at his mom. *"She's right. The cats, both of them, are afraid of disappointing her. She's like their queen or something."*

There was no way he was telling his mom that, but he had a feeling she knew already. He paced some more as Keith told him all he'd been able to find out about Em's family. It wasn't much, but it gave them a better picture of what she'd had to grow up with.

"They live in a house that belonged to a Theodore James, the same Jimmy that knew Rayne all those years ago. They've been living there since Em's mother was taken away. And as far as I can tell, the taxes are being paid on the house as well as any upkeep that needs to be taken care of."

"That would be because I had someone taking care of all the properties that I own. Jimmy's was no different." Peter bowed before them. "I do hate to show up uninvited, but I have news for you all. The brothers are now down to two, and the father...I thought I had convinced him that bringing Em back with them was a bad idea, but he has had a change of heart on the matter. I believe he wants to bring her to heel much more now. The second oldest has now killed another. I believe he was the baby of the family."

Em told Brock the name, and he relayed it to the room. "Erwin. Em said that he was younger than her by four years. She wants to know if Wilfred killed him as well."

"Yes. I'm afraid that he has. I do believe if this trend keeps up, you'll only have to deal with him when he gets here. And that should be very soon. The three police that were injured last night...they have no memory as to what happened to them, and I have put him someplace safe for now."

Brock looked at the vampire. "You're helping them kill each other off, aren't you? You're doing something to make them fight with each other and murder one another."

"In a way, I am. I'm simply telling them what is happening and giving them each enough information to blame another. I may have told a little lie to Wilfred when I spoke to him the first time, but since then...." He shrugged. "I have told them only what I know to be the truth. It will be easier on you if there is only one rather than the five, don't you think?"

"You think there will be more killings from them?" Brock looked at Jules as he asked, and nodded when Em and Peter did. "More humans, or will they kill more of them? Because I, for one, would like for there to be only one when they get here. I have enough to do without screwing around with a bunch of nut balls." Everyone laughed, as he was sure Jules had wanted them to.

"Both themselves and humans, I believe. They are getting hungry by now and will not stop until they get here. And before you ask, yes, I did take away their ability to feed on humans. Tonight when they rise, they will no longer be able to bite, if that urge has not been taken from them already. I should have thought of that sooner, but I didn't think about them killing for no other reason than because they could." He bowed again. "For that, I ask you for your forgiveness. The police officers would not have been so grievously hurt had I thought things through."

"But you saved them. And that's more of a chance than they had before I sent them there to be hurt." Em nodded at Brock and walked toward him as he continued. "The police, the ones you saved, Peter, were friends of mine with families. I had them watching the office so that the minute the alarm went off they could catch them in the act. I never dreamed they'd cut them down like that."

"But as you said, they are safe now. And they were cut down, but had I not intervened, then I'm afraid it would have been much worse. As it was, it was bad enough. How about we just say that both of us learned from our mistakes this night and be done with it for good?" Brock nodded.

"How long before you think they'll show up? I'm assuming that it will be soon since they attacked the lawyer's house tonight." Peter told Brock they would show when the sun set that night. "We'll be ready. They'll know to come here, so you all will go home and take Em with—"

"You finish that statement and I will take you to the wood shed." His mom punched her finger into his chest as she continued. "I should have taken you there more often than I did. Maybe you wouldn't have been so stupid as to believe that any of us would leave here knowing that those monsters are on their way."

"But, Mom, they're coming for—"

"I don't give a good fig what they think they're coming for. And that young woman isn't leaving your side, either." She turned and winked at Em before she turned on him again. "Of all my children, I thought you would have a lick of sense to know that we are a streak of tigers, not a single one that takes on more than he can chew and thinks he'll come out the other side. You listen to me, young man. It's all of us, or so help me, I will paddle your bottom but good."

Brock wasn't sure what to say to her. His mom could be a little intense, as Em had said about her when it suited her. Usually in board meetings and dealing with the public when she needed to, but she'd never been like that to him. When he opened his mouth to say he had this covered, Em spoke to him.

"If she doesn't kick your ass, I certainly will. What do you think you're going to do against three vampires that are stupid as they come all alone? Nothing, I tell you, because you won't be doing it alone if I have to beat you myself and make you let us help you."

He was outnumbered. As soon as Bronwyn and Ryland started on him, the rest of them joined in as well. Jules told him in no uncertain terms that he would be there, as did the rest of them. He did get some help from Ryland when Bronwyn said she'd be going, but in the end neither of them stood a chance when it came to convincing her she should stay at home. Of course, when she and Rayne pinned them against the wall with nothing more than their minds, it was a moot point after that. They were by far a better weapon than an enemy had on them any day.

Chapter 11

Wilfred found the house his sister was staying at. He was glad now that he'd had the stupid solicitor give him the address before he'd left them the other day. It was later than he'd wanted to get a start on getting Emma's ass home but now that he'd figured it out, he was ready to go. Going back to the house his dad had gotten for them before sunrise yesterday was perfect. He moved into the kitchen area to find his brother Shawn sitting in the kitchen with one of the people who had been in the house when he'd woken up this evening. Her throat had been cut open and his brother was watching the blood pour from her wound.

"I can't feed from her. I thought when I couldn't bite her that I could simply feed this way, but I can't. It's as if she's blocked from me." Shawn looked up at him and Wilfred could see his hunger. "Have you been able to feed at all?"

Wilfred nodded, but the truth was he'd not been able to either. And like Shawn had done, cutting the vein open hadn't worked either. As soon as his brother burst into tears, Wilfred wanted to take back his lie, but he didn't want to seem foolish in front of his little brother either.

"Things will work out when we return home." At least Wilfred hoped so. He kept thinking of what the other man had said to him about feeding and humans. He looked at his brother's throat and wondered if he could feed from him instead. When he licked his lips, he felt his fangs drop, ready to bite. But before he could move to his brother, his dad walked in the room.

"Finally. Christ, where have you been all night? We're fucking hungry and we can't figure out what the fuck is wrong. Do you think some of the blood we drank at that party was tainted?" Wilfred told him he didn't know. "Look at all that blood. Christ, I feel like I could bite anything that moved right now just to fill the empty hole in my belly."

Wilfred backed away from him. Not because he was afraid, he told himself, but because his dad was looking at his throat like it was his last meal. He was also aware that he was looking at him in much the same manner as he had Shawn, but felt his was different. He was only thinking about it, and his dad looked ready to act on his hunger.

"Stay the fuck away from me or I'll tear your throat out." His dad backed up as Wilfred glanced at Shawn. "Did you see that? He was going to bite me and drink from me. I'm betting that as soon as we go to rest, he'll tear our throats out and kill us."

"I was doing no such thing." His dad looked at Shawn, who had stood up now. "You can't think I'd do something like that to my own sons, can you?"

"I think you killed Steven too." His dad took a step back as Wilfred continued. "You were the only ones there when I went to bed. What happened after I went to the attic?"

"You killed him. You as much admitted it to me. If you didn't, then why did you go up to the attic? You slept in the basement before that. Why were you in the attic, of all places?" Shawn didn't say anything to their dad's rant. "Besides, you killed him and you know it. You never liked him anyway, and less when you all changed. You killed him and we know it."

He lunged at his dad. What he was saying was entirely too close to the truth and he wanted to shut him up before Shawn started to ask questions. He pulled his dad to his chest and held him tightly against him.

"You think you're so clever trying to get us to fight against each other when all along you've wanted Emma to yourself." Not true, because Wilfred wanted her all to his self. He exposed his dad's throat and watched as Shawn licked his lips. "You think we can feed off him, brother? Bite in deep and drink until we're full?"

"Stop this right now. I'm your father and you can't kill me." He reached out for Shawn. "Come on, son. Don't let him talk you into killing me. You know as well as I do that you don't want to do this. Not kill me when we know that Wilfred is the one causing all the problems around here. We need to think about what the other vampire told me and go back home and forget about Emma."

He'd spoken to the vampire, too? Wilfred tried to think if he'd mentioned this before and couldn't recall it. Wilfred wanted him to shut up before he told Shawn anything like he'd told him, if he'd told him that they could no longer feed because of the things that they'd done. He looked at Shawn and smiled.

He could see that Shawn was too hungry to care who he fed from so long as he got a meal. As Shawn moved closer, Wilfred could see his fangs had dropped and he was going to join him in killing their father. As soon as he was close enough to take his wrist, Wilfred bit down into his dad's throat and felt the hot blood fill his mouth.

There was a bitter taste to it, but after a few swallows all he could think about was how good it tasted and how hungry he'd been. He heard his brother suckle at Dad's wrist and knew they were having the same feelings. Fuck him being their dad, they were hungry. It was sort of his duty as their father to make sure they were well fed, he thought with humor. When their dad started to get weaker and his struggles subsided so he was less trouble to hold onto, Wilfred lifted his head and let him drop. Shawn was still drinking from his wrist when Wilfred walked to the dying woman and snapped her neck. He still couldn't feed from her, but he didn't care right now. They were full, and he wondered if he'd be able to feed from his sister tomorrow night. When Shawn stood up, he wiped the blood off his mouth and moaned.

"I need to fuck something." Wilfred nodded. "Let's go see if we can find someone and bring her back here. We'll share."

Like fuck they would, but Wilfred didn't say anything. But as it turned out they couldn't leave to go anywhere. The sun was just cresting the sky, and they had to stay indoors. Wilfred looked at Shawn.

"We'll get Emma tonight when the sun sets and go back to the mansion with her. We'll be back to normal by then and things will be perfect. She'll be our day watcher and also bring us our meals like Jimmy said a watcher does." Shawn nodded. "Then we'll be safe again, and it'll be much better because it'll just be the two of us."

Shawn smiled and nodded. Wilfred could only think that it wouldn't be the two of them, unless you counted Emma and him. There was no way that Shawn was going back with them unless it was to feed him along the way. He went to the basement to rest as the sun was making him exhausted, and wondered what their dear sister would say when she found out she was going to be his. Smiling, he knew she'd fight him and he didn't care. She would soon submit or she'd be as dead as the rest of them. Wilfred was as happy as he'd been since he'd been changed all those years ago. Things were starting to finally fall into place.

As he went to the darkest part of the basement, he thought of his sister again. He'd wanted her changed when he had been, but Jimmy couldn't do it when she'd hurt him. She'd nearly torn his throat out when he'd tired.

Wilfred had held her down while they stripped her naked. At first he'd not understood, as none of them had been naked. Then he watched Jimmy. He never raped Emma, but he had hurt her all over her body. He thought maybe he was trying to weaken her, but it didn't seem to be working. She'd fought them both all the way until Jimmy had lain over her, ready to bite. But she'd jerked from his grasp so quickly that he'd been startled and had left his throat open, and her hand was loose as well. When she'd clawed at Jimmy's throat and torn a part of it away, Wilfred had been so shocked that she'd been able to slip off the table they'd had her on and out the door before either of them could go after her. Not that Jimmy could. He was dying, and had grabbed him and bit him deep in his throat to drink.

"You belong to me now." Jimmy had said that over and over in his mind as he drank deeper and deeper from him. When he became weak and dizzy, Jimmy finally let him go, and he lay there knowing that the end was near, and with him only being a vampire for less than a day. When Jimmy had offered him his wrist, Wilfred had drank from

it greedily, and had felt the power of his blood as it filled him. Jimmy's own wounds healed as he watched.

"You belong to me now. More than the others, you belong to me forever and a day." He hadn't been sure what that had meant then or now. And before he could remember to ask him about it, he'd left them to go to his own home. Then later they'd felt Jimmy's death and he still had no answers. But now he thought it meant that he and Jimmy had connected on a higher level than the rest of them had, and that's what made him superior to them. He laid his head on the pillow he'd brought down and closed his eyes. Tomorrow he'd exact his revenge for his maker on his sister, and change her for him. He was so excited that he didn't think he'd sleep, but the sun was more powerful than his excitement. But something stirred in his mind, and he opened his eyes as a curl of fear settled around him.

"*You are going to pay for this.*" He sat up and looked around the empty area. "*Did you really think that killing your own kind would go unnoticed? You had to know that you'd not be able to kill and kill without facing the consequences. You are not that stupid, are you? But then again, you probably are.*"

"Who are you? What the hell do you want?" He saw a shadow and stared at it as he solidified into a man. "You're the vampire from the other day. What the fuck do you want with me? I've done nothing to you. What are you?

"Your maker's maker. I'm the one that gave you life when there was none before." The man moved so close that Wilfred could almost feel the breath on his face; see the color of his eyes as they filled with the ruby redness of blood. "You're going to pay, Wilfred Robin Cole, pay like none have paid before."

Then he was alone. Wilfred lay back on his bed and tried to think what the hell had just happened. He tried to convince himself that he'd just killed his dad and it was playing tricks on his mind. That he'd drank from another vampire, and the bitter taste it had given him was just that, tainted blood. He lay back down and nearly convinced himself that what had just happened hadn't and he was just tired. Then something touched his face and he screamed.

~~~

Viktor showed up just after the hottest part of the day had started to cool. Em had seen him on the porch and had gone to see what he wanted. He touched her mind, and she felt comfort from him but didn't trust him.

"I am Viktor Ravengric, fifth son of Viktor Ravengric and Katja Ravengric." He bowed before her. "*You are the child which I have come to protect, I believe. The one I have heard a great many things about. All good, I assure you.*"

She stepped back for him, and he shook his head. Then she remembered that he couldn't enter unless someone invited him. And she suddenly decided that she liked that idea. She wondered if her brothers could enter hers and Brock's home without her permission.

"*No, they cannot, my child. Someone would have to invite them verbally, and then only the persons who reside in the house permanently.*" He bowed again. "*I am sorry, my lady, but if you could summon Peter, I would be most appreciative. He is aware of me coming here.*"

Summon Peter. She had no idea how to do that. But she did know how to summon the others. She reached for Brock and all the rest and asked them to come to the house. She told them who was there and what he wanted her to do. Bronwyn was the first to answer her.

"He's telling you the truth, but don't invite him in until I get there. Gabby and I were just on our way back home and I can be there in less than two minutes." She felt her laughter. "You're a smart cookie. Anyone ever tell you that before?"

"No. Not that I can ever remember. And I'm...I'm afraid, Bronwyn. What if they come here, somehow get someone to invite them in, and they kill us in our sleep?" Her laughter again pissed Em off. "Why is this funny?"

"Because, my dear sister, you are one bad-assed bitch, and once they get a load of those cats of yours, they are going to shit themselves." Bronwyn had a way with words that still amazed her. "We're in the driveway now. And I think Peter is on his way as well. He can get into your house, so he might – "

A movement in her peripheral vision startled her, and she turned to see Peter standing there. She told Bronwyn, and she laughed again. By the time her heart began to slow, Em could see her big SUV pulling up to the garage. Things were about to get a whole lot scarier if the man standing at the door wasn't who he said he was.

"Master." Peter let her hear what he was saying, and she was grateful for it. When he nodded to her, she turned to let him and Bronwyn in, but Viktor hesitated before stepping over the threshold.

"You're much stronger than we first thought, aren't you, my dear?" Em looked at Peter, who was still standing next to her. She looked back at the man who smiled. She had a feeling that Peter and Viktor were talking about her, and it made her a little mad. When Gabby was put into her arms suddenly, she looked at Bronwyn.

"It's hard to stay pissy when she's around. Look at her and focus on her smile." She looked down at the baby. "Calm the beast, Em. She's mad and wants out."

Em felt her then. She was clawing at her to be released, and she took deep breaths to try and get her to stay where she was. When the baby in her arms moved, she looked down at her and looked into her eyes. There was something there, a spark of something that made Em feel calmer, and the more she and the baby stared at one another, the calmer she became. When the little girl yawned, so did Em. And then the baby smiled at her. Bronwyn was right; it was hard to stay mad with her in her arms.

She could feel Brock coming closer, but also her brother, Wilfred. And...she thought it was Shawn, but it was hard for her to focus long enough to figure it out. Wilfred's anger was making her cat stir again, but for a different reason. She looked at the two vampires, Viktor still on the outside of the house and Peter just in front of him. They both turned to her.

"He's near, and he has Shawn." Both men nodded. *"Can he come in? I know it's not my house, but I stay here. I don't want him to be able to come in, but can he make me let him?"*

"It must be verbal, love." She flushed, embarrassed that because of her handicap she couldn't invite the man in after he'd agreed to help her. Peter lifted her chin so she could see him. "My master is not making fun of you, nor is he thinking of what has happened to you as a handicap. He knew that you'd been injured when he came here. And what happened to you didn't make you weak, but a strong woman who's been able to thwart her very powerful brothers for all this time and come out on top every time. You should be proud of what you've done, not embarrassed because you cannot invite an old turd like him into your home." Viktor smiled at her, and she smiled back. He'd done it again, made her feel comfortable. He stood on the porch while she went to the kitchen to get herself a cup of hot tea and one for Bronwyn as well.

She thought about all the things she'd been able to do since coming here. She'd gotten a good job and made a great many friends. And she'd found her mate. Thinking about Brock made her remember this morning, after his family had left, and what they had done. He'd taken her to the woods behind his house and had shown her what tigers could do.

"When you shift you should try to have a set of clothes nearby so you can change. If you can strip down, great. But when there is no time, your clothes get shredded when you shift. Your cat is much bigger than your human self, and clothes aren't that sturdy."

She nodded as he took off his shirt. Every time the man took off anything, she was suddenly all hot and bothered. She looked up at his face when his hand suddenly stilled at the waist of his pants.

"You're not making these lessons go very well if you look at me like that." She didn't really care for lessons so much as she wanted to watch him strip. She licked her lips, and he groaned.

"You should show me how you strip off your clothes. You said that these lessons would be very thorough. I need to know everything." She watched as he slid his hands into his pants, and watched as he cupped his balls. "You're not stripping."

"I know, but I'm enjoying myself thinking about your cat this morning. How sleek and beautiful you looked. And thinking about how when you do shift, I'm going to take you to the ground and fuck you as a cat." He moved his other hand to his cock, and she took a step toward him. "That's it, baby, come here and help me."

"You are doing just fine the way you are. But I want to see you." She knelt down in the dirt and pulled his soft pants off, and moaned at what she'd unveiled. "You're so beautiful, and I want to taste you."

152

His hiss of approval made her wet. She licked his cock from balls to tip and suckled the pearl of cum at the tip. When he wrapped his fingers into her hair, she took him deep into her mouth and swirled her tongue around the thick crown of him and cupped his ass.

"Put your hand on my balls and hold them." She did as he asked and loved the weight of them in her hands. *"Christ, baby if you keep that up, I'm going to come down your throat and not inside of you like we both want."*

She let his cock go when he pulled her head back. She reached for him, and he shook his head. When he took a step back from her, she stood up and took off her shirt. If he wouldn't come in her mouth, then she would have to get him to come some other way. As soon as she had tossed off her bra, then pulled off her pants and panties at the same time, she looked at him. There was nothing more beautiful than him.

"Shift for me." She closed her eyes at his request and let her tiger take her. The other cat was just there. She wanted out as well, but Em could feel her sitting back and waiting her turn. As soon as she opened her eyes, it took her several seconds to focus on the large tiger in front of her.

Snarling at him, she took off for the deeper woods. She wasn't very stealthy at her running yet, but she was having fun. Twice he leapt at her, and she took a tumble but got up quickly and started running again. When he caught up with her the third time, he sank his teeth into her shoulder and held her down.

Her cat hadn't liked that and snarled at him. Her beast, as she'd taken to calling the other cat, snarled as well, and seemed to run along her skin. Brock's cat felt it as well, she could tell, and when he roared at her, she let the beast go.

"Mother fuck." He bit her harder and she moaned. *"She's more beautiful than your other cat. And mine wants her."*

He mounted her from behind, and she lifted her ass up for him. His beast wasn't as gentle as Brock was when he wanted to be, nor was he happy when Em's beast tried to bite him back. When he entered her, she knew that he didn't care at all if she got any pleasure out of their sex, and snarled at him again.

"When he comes, I'm going to shift and fuck you like you've never been fucked before." She moaned. *"Then I'm going to do it again for good measure."*

His strokes were hard, quick, and almost painful. When he lifted his teeth from her flesh, she felt his tongue lick along the wound and moaned. When he did it again, she felt the stirring of a climax and begged him to do it again. When his teeth entered her other shoulder, it was gentle and almost erotic. He licked her twice when he let her go, and she came apart. He roared out his own release as he bit her again.

"Shift, love. Now, so I can finish us both." But she hadn't wanted finished. She wanted more, and when she shifted, she stayed where she was and Brock covered her as a human. *"You like this, don't you? You like being taken as an animal."*

She moaned when he entered her, and she wrapped her hand around his when he'd pinched her clit. Her climax this time was soft and smooth, almost an afterthought to the powerful one she'd had before.

When he suddenly lifted from her body, she was on her back before she could form a thought. As soon as his mouth took her clit, she screamed out in her mind over and over as she came. These were far from gentle, but like he was pulling them from her one at a time and right on top of each other. She was drained when he made his way up her body, biting and nipping at her oversensitive flesh.

He entered her slowly, filling her with his cock as he kissed her. He kissed his way to her shoulder as he moved in and out of her slowly, seemingly taking his time now that he had her. She wrapped her ankles around his hips, and he buried himself deeper still.

"I love you." She nodded, incapable of any thought but how good he was making her feel, how sated she was now that she'd come. *"And I want to spend the rest of my life showing you how much I love you."*

"I love you, too, Brock. I think I always have." She kissed his shoulder and then licked his skin. *"You taste so good to me. I don't think I could ever get enough of you."*

"Bite me, love. Let a little of your tiger go and mark me as yours." She felt her beast race to the front, and she knew that moment he felt her. *"Let her mark me as well. Bite me, love. Bite me while I come."*

As soon as her beast took her, she let her lick his skin, too. Her approval made Em ache for more, and when she sank her teeth deep into his muscle, Em came, fracturing into thousands of pieces only to do it again when he bit her as well.

When he lifted his head, she looked up, and her body tightened again when she saw the blood drip from his lips. When he threw back his head, she knew that he was roaring out his release, and put her hand to his chest to feel it. That alone had thrown her over the edge again and into darkness. She went willingly, knowing that he'd keep her safe so long as he lived.

When someone touched her arm, she pulled from her memory to look at them. Sandra was standing there with a glass of tea. Em took it, too embarrassed at being caught by

Brock's mom thinking about the most fantastic sex she'd ever had.

"I'm not even going to ask you what you were thinking about." Em felt her face heat as she drained the glass. She looked at the others in the room and realized that everyone was there. And Brock was coming toward her. When he sat down, he took her hand and kissed it. She watched as he slipped a diamond on her finger.

"I forgot to give you this last night." She looked at the ring, then back at him. "You said you'd marry me. Well, not in so many words, but when you came seven times, I figured all those 'yeses' one of them had to be for my question."

"You're nuts. But yes, I did say I'd marry you." She looked around the room. "Will they be upset that you've taken on a wife that is handicapped like — ?"

"You say that word again and I will beat your ass. And trust me, it won't be as enjoyable as it was the last time. I'll not let you come until you promise not to say it again." She nodded, and he laughed. "You'll say it again just to spite me, won't you?"

She nodded again. She loved this man very much and couldn't wait until this was finished so she could show him again and again how much she really and truly did. She felt him stiffen and looked at him.

"They're here."

Chapter 12

Wilfred entered the property without any problems. He had anticipated them after the evening he'd had so far. Everything was going to shit, and he was a little afraid that this wasn't going to go just as he'd hoped either. He glanced at his brother, who still looked a little shocked.

"You did the right thing." Shawn nodded but still didn't speak. "I didn't know that you had to stake vampires even if they had been drained. Did you?"

Shawn still didn't speak, like he hadn't since they'd done what had to be done. Or at least he'd done what had to be done. Shawn had saved Wilfred's life, he was sure of it. But now...now the man looked like he wished he hadn't. Thinking about what had happened made him shiver, and he was afraid all over. He hated that feeling but didn't know how to get over it like he'd been telling Shawn to do.

Their dad had still been alive when they'd entered the kitchen that evening. He was weak, Wilfred supposed, but he'd been strong enough to attack him as soon as he'd walked into the room. And when he had, Wilfred had been so surprised that he'd not been able to fight back until it was almost too late. But by then his father was holding him in a way that he couldn't get away from.

"You tried to kill me," his dad had said. "You can't kill your own father. That's like every rule in the world."

The sharpened pencil was coming closer and closer to his heart, and Wilfred was terrified that he was going to kill him with it. Then his dad stiffened and, suddenly, flames burst from his chest. Wilfred had watched in abject horror as the man who had fathered him was suddenly gone. He looked up to see his brother standing over him.

"You saved me." The piece of wood that Shawn had in his hand dropped to the floor, making a loud noise in the otherwise quiet room. "How could he still be alive after we drank from him last night? How is it possible that he survived the day after what we'd done to him?"

Shawn didn't say anything but had turned and left the room. Wilfred stood, thinking to go after him, but he wasn't sure what to say. Somehow he didn't think that telling him thanks would go over that well, and he stayed in the kitchen until it was time to leave. Going into the living room, he'd found Shawn huddled on the floor with a blanket around his shoulders.

Shawn had aged a great deal since the incident with their dad, and Wilfred was worried. He wouldn't kill his brother now, even though that had been his plan when he'd gotten up. He might need him again sometime, and it was always good to have someone at your back, especially when it was your brother who had proven himself as someone who would save him already.

The drive over to the house where he knew his sister was staying was made in silence. When they pulled into the drive, they found the gates open and drove through them as if they were a welcomed guest. Wilfred smiled, thinking they were anything but that. He was surprised to see only one truck in the drive, because he'd assumed that she'd know he was coming for her. Wilfred thought the other vampire would have told her everything. The vampire knew a great deal about a lot of stuff, including them, and that made him uncomfortable. When he opened his car door, Shawn got out as well.

"We're going to get her and get the hell out." Shawn only stared at him with a blank look. "Are you going to be helpful, or are you going to just get in my way?"

Still no answer, but he did move up to the front door. Wilfred stood where he was and got his first good look at the house. Christ, it was as big as five or six of the houses that they'd lived in before coming here.

Brick with tall columns held up what looked to him like another balcony on the upper level. The six columns were decorated with large hanging baskets that spilled over with vines and bright colorful flowers. The front steps were made of a light marble and fanned out from the front door about twenty feet that flowed out into the drive and yard like it was all one piece. He admired the dozen or so chairs and tables that were spread out in groupings under windows that had baskets at them as well. The windows were open and he could see a slight breeze move the curtains.

He sneered at his sister's apparent wealth, and it made him all the more determined to bring her to heel when he got her home. She was more than likely a whore for the man that owned this house, or his maid. But knowing her like he thought he did, she was probably both. She'd be wiping up his fucking crumbs while he fucked her from behind. Wilfred pounded on the door and yelled for Emma, not even thinking about the fact she couldn't hear him.

When the door was opened, he almost took a step back. Christ, she was beautiful. More beautiful than she'd been when they had lived together. In fact, the only reason he knew it was her was because of the scar that was on her throat. She smiled at him, and he reached for her.

His entire arm felt as if he'd rammed it against a concrete wall. He staggered back, holding his arm, and tried to step into the house. He was thrown back just as he realized someone needed to invite him in. Her smile broadened.

"You think this is funny, you fucking bitch? Wait until we get you back to the house. Invite me in now, or so help me it won't go well for you when I do come in." She shook her head. "You heard me, invite me in."

Another woman appeared next to his sister, and he couldn't take his eyes off her. Where his sister's beauty was soft and natural, this woman looked like a spread in one of his magazines he got monthly, with ruby red lips and full large breasts. His cock hardened when he tried to think of her naked and spread out before him. When she smiled, Wilfred thought he'd died and gone to heaven. He had to try three times before he could tell her what he wanted.

"This is my sister, Emma Cole. She needs to come out so we can take her back home. Could you please invite us in so we can discuss the details?" He felt his smile fade when the woman laughed at him. "She's our sister, and we'd like to take her home. Now, bitch."

"Oh, and you were doing so well before. And you can fuck yourself. You're not coming in unless she says you can, and as you know, it has to be a verbal invite and I'm pretty sure you're not going to get that from her." The woman looked at Emma, then back at him. "She wants me to translate for her. She said you guys never learned to speak sign language. Were you too good to learn how to communicate with your own sister, you moron?"

Wilfred snorted and tried his best not to get pissed any more than he was already. "She'll learn to talk or live in silence. She's not going to get any special treatment from us. Tell her to get her shit together and come out so we can get back before the sun comes up."

He thought he heard her call him a moron again but wasn't sure. He saw something move within the house but knew that couldn't be right. A tiger inside the house? No fucking way.

"She said to tell you no." He waited for more, but apparently she wasn't going to say anything else, so he snarled at her. "You think you scare me, big boy? I got news for you. I've killed men a great deal stronger than you with nothing but a thought. You're nothing more than a flea on the back of a camel's ass. Your sister said no, so I think this ends our conversation."

The door shut in his face, and he stood there for several seconds just waiting for it to open again. This couldn't be happening. There was no way this fucking bitch had just slammed the door in his face. He looked at Shawn, who was smiling.

"So now you have a sense of humor?" Shawn nodded and leaned against the house. But when he looked out over the drive behind him, Wilfred saw him stiffen. Closing his eyes before turning, Wilfred just knew it wasn't going to be his sister with all her bags sitting around her ready to go. Turning slowly, he nearly fell back against the house when he saw them.

Nine of the biggest fucking tigers he'd ever seen were standing there staring at them, and the one in the middle looked like he'd been on steroids all his life, as he was nearly twice the size of the others. Wilfred whimpered when the big one took a few steps forward and stopped. A man came with Em from the side of the house, and stood on either side of the tiger.

"Hello, Wilfred and Shawn Cole. My name is Peter Oliver." He smiled, and Wilfred saw his fangs. "You've been very bad children, and it's time to put an end to all this madness."

"You're the man from the other night." Peter bowed. "You said you were Jimmy's maker and that we're now your children."

"I did, and you are. What have you to say about the crimes you've committed? Something surely. You've been killing since the night you were changed, and it has only gotten worse since then." Peter looked to his left as another man came forward. "This is my maker, and he will sentence you. Then justice will be—"

"Wait a fucking minute here. Sentence me for what? We had to feed, didn't we? We can't just go to the local store and get a bag of blood to eat from." Wilfred looked at his brother, who still hadn't said a word. "He's all the family I have left aside from my sister, and I'd very much like to forget this whole thing and take Emma home with me. Besides, Jimmy told us you can't kill your children unless someone allows it."

"Miss Emma isn't going anywhere with you. As a matter of fact, you won't be leaving either. And I won't be doing the killing. My maker will, or you'll be given to these cats." Peter looked at the cats behind him and put his hand on the one beside him. "I think in order for justice to be served you should be killed by these men and woman. You have made their lives a little on the difficult side for a long time."

"Give us to them? You mean serve them?" Peter laughed and shook his head. Wilfred looked at his sister, then at the cats, as what the man was saying dawned on him. "You want them to kill us? You think to let them tear us apart and we're just supposed to let them? That so ain't going to happen. Not so long as I can fight back."

"Oh, they want you to fight back. They love it when their prey runs and tries to hide from them. Ryland explained to me once that the blood runs hotter when they run. You've not fed for a while except from your father, of course, but you should have enough for them to feast on, I would think." Peter nodded to his sister, and she smiled. "She's going to go after you first. After all, you caused her the most harm, wouldn't you say?"

The shift was sudden. Where his sister had stood now stood a large tiger. And when she opened her mouth, he could see the mouthful of sharp, long teeth that he was sure she meant to tear into him with. He took a step back and fell against the door that had been slammed in his face not moments ago.

The large cat that had stood beside her now rubbed himself against her, and Wilfred had a sudden and clear thought. His sister was a shifter. And according to Jimmy, her blood would be so wonderful that it would get them high. He knew, too, because he'd had a shifter recently. He looked at the man next to Peter.

"You can kill my brother. He'll be payment enough for whatever it is you think we've done." He glanced at Shawn, who was staring at him. "You go out there and let them kill you, and I'll take Emma home. You'll see, it'll all work out."

"You think I'm just going to nod and let them tear me to pieces for shit I had little to do with?" Wilfred nodded, not understanding what the problem was. "You're insane. I'm not going to do it...not willingly anyway. Oh, I'm guilty, but you're stupid if you think to sacrifice me for you to go away without any kind of punishment."

"I'm the oldest now that Steven is dead, and I make the rules. Get your ass out there and let them do what they need to so that this can be finished." Peter cleared his throat. "What the fuck is it now? You want your pound of flesh, and I'm giving it to you. Shawn will go out and do whatever you need—"

"I'm afraid you don't understand, Wilfred...you're both going to die. Either by this streak of tigers or by...other means." Peter looked at the other man again. "His way will be much quicker and a great deal less painful."

Shawn took a step off the porch and walked to them. Wilfred was glad he was seeing things his way finally and looked at his sister. She wasn't going to make it home. He would drain her before they left the state. Licking his lips and feeling his fangs drop into place, he looked over at his brother as he stood in front of the other man.

"I wish to die by your hand." Wilfred thought he'd heard him wrong, but when the other man lifted his hand and touched him, Shawn was ash raining to the ground as if he'd been that all along. Mother fuck, that was quick. And now they all looked at him.

"Jimmy should have trained us better." Peter snorted. "He told us the rules, but he didn't tell us that we couldn't break them."

That sounded stupid even to his own ears. Apparently to Peter and the other man as well, because they both laughed. The large male cat made his way toward him as his sister made her way to his left. They were going to try and make him run, but he was smarter than any ignorant shifter was.

"One more chance, Wilfred. Do you die by their hand or by my master's?" Peter crossed his arms over his chest. "I hope you decide on the cats. I would love to see what they can do to you in a short period of time. And for your sister this will be a training tool. She's not had much opportunity to hunt yet."

That sent a shiver down his spine, and he looked at his sister. Christ, she was going to kill him. Fear compounded into more fear until he could feel the sweat run down his spine and the need to flee pounding at him. He looked at his car and decided that if he could get to it, he'd be safe. Almost as soon as he thought it, two of the big cats sliced the tires open with their large claws, and then his car flipped over onto its top. He didn't have to look at Peter to know that he'd read his mind and had destroyed his only means of escape. When pain ripped through his leg, he looked down at the male cat. He'd torn his flesh open and was licking the blood from his paw. Wilfred couldn't help it; he took off for the woods.

~~~

The woods were dense, but Brock knew them as well as he did his own home. As he moved deeper into the woods, following—but not too closely—the animal they were chasing, he thought of what he'd been told about the man whose scent he was chasing.

"He tied me to the table in the kitchen and left me there all day. I was so exhausted from running the day before that I slept off and on. I'd escaped and had tried to get as much distance between me and them as I could, but they caught me easily enough. Dad said it was because my scent called to him." Em had snuggled closer to him, but he had a feeling she was

more there than with him. *"At first I thought they were just going to hold me there until I agreed to be their sort of watcher. They needed me to watch the house and stuff."*

Brock knew what a day watcher was, and it was more than just watching the house that the vampires resided in. She would bring them back humans to feed from, and be there for them herself if none was available for them. And when the mood struck them, be their sexual partner, whether she wanted it or not.

"But then Jimmy showed up just before they rose. He was looking at me as if I was a fine meal that they'd laid out for him and he was going to feast. He'd just sat down when my dad came into the room, and he watched Jimmy as he tore off my clothes. I didn't know what was going to happen so I just watched, screaming at them to leave me alone in my head." He held her tighter.

"When he stood over me and...he fondled me, I tried to get away. Wilfred came in with the others, and I could see that they were fine with whatever was going to happen. When Wilfred held my head in his hands, I just knew that he was going to bite me, but Jimmy leaned down and...."

To have that happen to her was bad enough, but to not know, to not be able to hear or even to scream must have been terrifying for her. He watched her as tears rolled down her face, and he listened to what she'd done.

"I was trying to grab for anything to use as a weapon, but there was nothing. His teeth were so sharp, and I screamed over and over, begging him to stop, when suddenly my hand found a fork that had been on the table. I pulled it up and stabbed Jimmy in the face as many times as I could before I was let go. I left the house and never looked back." She looked at him. *"I thought I'd killed him, but I guess I didn't."*

"No. Peter and his maker did that for crimes against his kind. I guess Jimmy was the one who had set up the labs that had

changed both Rayne and Bronwyn. He was funding them, and Peter found out. I don't know what they did to him, but I'm pretty sure he's gone now." In fact Brock was sure of it, because when he'd heard that the scar on her neck had come from Jimmy, he asked Peter if he could have ten minutes alone with the prick. And now he was chasing the other bastard who'd hurt his love.

His scent was getting stronger, and he moved toward it. He'd opened his leg up, but figured by now the vampire had had time to heal. He had hoped that he'd bleed so badly that he'd die, but Brock knew that he wanted to play with him a bit more. When he saw his brother, he had blood on his muzzle.

"He's over near the pond. I think he's hiding in one of the hollowed-out logs there." Ryland snorted. *"The man is beyond stupid. Doesn't he know that we're going to catch him anyway?"*

"I think he believes that he is still more powerful than us, even if he hasn't fed and has lost a great deal of blood." Brock watched Wilfred run by them, making enough noise to wake the dead. *"And I agree with you about his stupidity. You'd think he'd be better equipped to handle something like this."*

When Em moved next to him, Ryland faded into the forest. She rubbed her head over his shoulder. He asked her if she was doing all right.

"I thought it would be easy to kill him. To make him pay for all the things he's done to me and thought about doing, but I can't do it. It's like I see him still as my older brother and not this monster he's become." He nodded. His brothers were his life, as were their mates. And now he had his own and would put her safety ahead of theirs no matter what. He lifted his nose to the air when he scented Wilfred on the move again.

"You stay here and I'll find him and take care of this. I wouldn't be able to kill one of my brothers either, I don't think,

no matter what kind of crime they committed. All right, love?" She nodded, and he rubbed over her again. *"You're my life, and when this is over, we'll go on a nice long vacation and forget all about what happens here today."*

He moved toward the vampire and found him easily enough. Before he could flush him out of the bushes he was hiding in, his beast surged forward and took him. Brock lay there for several seconds while he tried to regain control, but he wasn't having it. He reached for his family.

"I'm not myself." Jules said no shit and laughed. *"I don't know what he's going to do, and I haven't any control. You have to leave the forest now and take Em with you."*

He saw two of his brothers leap out from behind trees not ten feet from him. Then he saw Jules and Ally move from the opposite direction. He was ready to move again when he felt something hit him hard in the back. He rolled over, head over ass, twice before he saw Wilfred over him with a large log. As he was coming at him again, Brock started to stand, but was knocked back by Em. Her beast had come out to play as well. And she looked ready to tear Wilfred apart.

Chapter 13

Em snarled at Wilfred. She wanted him to drop the log and back the fuck up, but he swung it at her again. When she lifted her paw at him, she was able to tear at his leg again before he tried to hit her. Brock roared at her to stand down, and she roared back.

"*Mine.*" Brock stood up and towered over her for several seconds before he dropped back down and roared again. She screamed at him this time. "*Mine. He's mine or I kick your ass.*"

She could almost see his face. His brow would be lifted and he'd have that snotty grin on his face. She turned her back on him and looked at her brother. He had hurt what was hers and now he had to pay.

"Are you Emma?" She stopped advancing on Wilfred when he asked her. "The reason I'm asking is because you should know that I don't want to die."

She sat down and watched him. He hadn't let go of the log yet, but he wasn't holding it up like he was going to hurt anyone either. She didn't believe for one minute that he was going to drop it and leave without hurting her. And even if he did, she wasn't going to let him. She cocked her head at him when he began to speak, just realizing that she could understand him.

"You're not human right now, not even a shifter." Viktor's voice poured over her and felt like she was in the warm sunshine and a bed of flowers at the same time. *"You should also know that so long as your beast is taking you that you'll be immune to all sorts of pains that your brother will try to inflict on you."*

"You mean he can't hit me?" That sounded almost too good to be true, and when he spoke again, she knew it was. But Viktor didn't make her feel childish or stupid because she'd not understood him.

"Nay, child, he can hit you, but as your beast you'll not feel them quite so badly." She felt something more from him and started to ask him about it when her brother spoke.

"Are you listening to me, or are you faking not being able to hear me?" He leaned on the log. "I didn't hurt you all that badly, you know. All I wanted to do was to make you stop crying. All you ever did was cry."

"And that was a reason to kill me?" He looked at her oddly, and she realized he could hear her too. *"You're standing there trying to bargain your life with me when as a child you tried to drown me. Even today you were going to take me back to your home and convert me to something that I have no desire to be, and make me be your slave for the rest of my days. You seriously think that I should simply let you walk away?"*

"Of course you should. It's not like I succeeded in drowning you. Shit, Emma, you're still alive, aren't you? What the fuck do you want to hurt me over that for?" She could only stare at him and wonder how they had the same parents. "You should have stayed put when Jimmy was going to change you. None of those other people would have been hurt had you just minded me."

"You mean about quitting school when I was sixteen, or when you brought that man to the house to change me to a

vampire? Or is it when you said I should get my ass in the car and go back with you today?" As he'd never answered those questions, she repeated because she really wanted to know.

"I needed you to quit school for a very good reason. You were needed at the house to keep the house clean. It was a mess, and you know it's only gotten worst since you ran off. The only room in the house that was clean was yours when you lived there, and how fair was that?" She shook her head at him. "And Jimmy agreed with me on keeping you as a watcher. You would still have had to keep the house clean, but since we'd be sleeping all day, you had plenty of time. You're still coming back with me, Emma. And think how much easier the house will be to keep up with just me to look after."

"I'm not going anywhere with you, Wilfred. I'm in love with my mate and he and I are going to stay here forever." He didn't look happy, but she didn't care. Maybe if she made him realize she was serious, he'd simply go away or something.

"Why are you so selfish?" That shocked her. She'd never been selfish a day in her life as far as she knew, and never to him. He was always taking and taking. "You always have to have things just perfect or you won't budge. Well, I have needs and you're going to help me with them."

"Or what?" She looked over at Brock when he spoke to them both. *"She'll either do what you say, or what will you do to her? Kill her? Over my dead body, and I'm not going to be an easy man to go down."*

"You think? I'm pretty powerful. Jimmy said he'd never met a vampire as strong as me. He said...I can't remember, but he said I was going to go far with him."

"And where is he now? He's ash. Nothing more than a small pile of trash that was more than likely kicked away as soon as he was gone." Em noticed that two tigers were behind her brother, and she wondered what they were trying to do.

"They're here to protect you and nothing more. If you want him, he's yours to do with as you want. They know that." She looked over at Brock. *"They'll let you take care of him if you want, or we will. Either way, we're not leaving you here alone with this monster."*

She loved these people. All of them. When Bronwyn stood just to her other side, she turned to look at the beautiful tiger. Em knew that at that moment that she, too, would die for these people who had given her what she'd wanted all her life. She looked at Wilfred and realized he'd never been anything to her, not even before he'd been changed.

"You're going to die. And when you do, I'm not going to think of you ever again. And if I do, it will not be with fond memories, but with hatred and disdain. If you had given me one thimble full of the love I have for my new family, I would have helped you. But now...." She shook her head. *"Now you're nothing."*

When he lifted the log again, she stood up. The hair on her back seemed to dance along her skin, and she felt her beast race toward the surface. She let her take her, and in turn her brother. As soon as she leapt forward, Em knew that he was dead.

Blood filled her mouth as she tore at him. Muscles seemed to snap in two as she clawed at him. And the entire time, she was a bystander in her own body. She never felt the way her teeth sank into his throat, but saw the destruction. She didn't feel the moment his leg shattered under another bite, but did see it fly through the air and land several feet from them. His screams seemed so distant, so low that she barely heard them as he begged her. When his head rolled away, landing not a foot from her mate, she looked up at him and knew that he was proud of her. When the head rolled away from him, Brock stopped it with his paw, and they both watched as it incinerated, turned to ash, as his body did moments later.

When he was gone, not even a stain on the forest floor, she threw back her head and roared. And as the others joined her, she heard them, heard them tell anything within a few miles that something had happened, something huge had gone down.

Moving away from the place where she'd killed the monster, she went to Brock and noticed that the others had faded away. She didn't care right now, not when she was where she needed to be. Brock moved to stand over her when she lay down. Laying down her head, she closed her eyes, knowing that no matter what happened he would protect her. Sleep didn't just roll over her but took her hard and fast to where nothing mattered, and dreams were nothing she had to be afraid of any longer.

~~~

Brock watched her sleep. She'd not moved overly much since he'd put her to bed over three hours ago, but he wasn't worried. She'd killed her demon today, and now she needed to rest. And as long as she needed, he'd watch over her. He looked up when his mom came in the room after a quick knock.

"Bronwyn said that she wasn't dreaming. She was worried, but I guess she talked to Viktor and now she's fine with it." She leaned back in the chair. "Do you suppose she's been fighting them for so long she can now finally rest?"

He told her that he thought so. "When she is strong enough, we're going to take a long trip. Viktor has said we can use his villa in Paris and stay as long as we want. I want her to see some of the world before we have a family."

He looked at her again, knowing that she was going to be his for a very long time. Viktor had blessed them with the gift of life for their help in taking care of the Coles. He also said not to be surprised when she woke to find that her beast had made some changes in her body.

"I'm going to take her shopping." Brock looked at his mom. "Have you seen what she's been wearing? It's all well and good to wear your clothes around the house, but, Brock, you cannot expect her to wear your boxers and tee-shirts when she goes into town or to work. The poor girl doesn't even have a decent pair of boots."

"I'll take her." His mom huffed at him. "You don't think I can buy her clothes? I'll have you know that I've been disrobing women now for a long time, and I know what I like."

"Yes, I'm sure you do, but she won't be wearing negligees to work or to the grocery store. She'll need to wear things that will make her look beautiful, and not the kind you're thinking of buying that look good on the floor near your bed." He flushed. "You didn't think I'd ever forget finding your music teacher's panties in your room, did you?"

"She was just admiring my instrument." He laughed when his mom hit him. "I'm serious. You bought me that really nice trumpet and she wanted to see it. What did you think I meant?"

"First of all, you played the clarinet, not the trumpet, and secondly, what did that have to do with her leaving her panties behind?"

"She was...polishing it for me." Another slap and he laughed harder. "Ah Mom, you know just what was going on. We were having sex, and she was teaching me things that I couldn't get in sex education."

"Just wait until you have a daughter of your own. I swear to you when she starts pulling the same crap on you that you did to me, I'm going to sit back and laugh until I keel over." She handed him a sheath of papers he'd not noticed before. "Viktor pulled some strings, and had her family declared dead. Her mom is still in an institution and her bills are being paid by some vampire council because they're taking part of the blame for what happened to her. You think she'll want to see her mom after all this time?"

He looked over the papers briefly and then at his mom. "It'll be up to her. I'll do what she wants about her. If she wants to or not, she's all the family she has left."

After his mom left, he looked over the papers more thoroughly. The house that her family had gotten from Jimmy was now hers, as was the money that had been in their account. All the taxes were being paid by a third party, and Brock had a feeling the party was Peter. The man had apologized to him several times in the last several hours. Then as if he had summoned him, the man walked in.

"She's resting well, so I would like to speak to you for a moment or two if you wouldn't mind." Bronwyn walked in with Gabby and sat down. "She has agreed to sit with her for me so that we may talk." They moved to his office so they wouldn't disturb Em.

"If you tell me how sorry you are again, I swear to you that I will knock you on your ass. I get it, you're sorry about what Jimmy did. Well, so am I, but I certainly don't blame you. I blame those idiots that came here after her." Peter nodded and sat in the chair across from him. He looked over his desk and noticed that someone had been using his computer.

"It was me. We needed to get the ball rolling for Em to inherit, and the computer was the quickest way. Your brother Keith was very helpful."

Brock nodded and waited. When Viktor walked in, he stood up. There was something about the older vampire that inspired one to be very formal. Brock sat when he did.

"I would like for you to work for me." That took him by surprise, but before he could comment, Viktor continued, "Our vampire council has a great many rogues like Wilfred and his family that need to be taken care of. You and your lovely mate would be perfect for the job."

"You gave us the ability to live forever and now you want your payback?" Brock didn't know what to think when Viktor shook his head. "Then what is it? You don't have enough vampires that you need to hire a few tigers to do it for you?"

"Oh, we have enough vampires. Too many we think at times, but no, that's not it. We want to hire you because of your third tigers." Brock looked at Peter. "He didn't tell me about him and her, but I felt them. Do you know how long it has been since I've felt that sort of strength? Longer than your earth has been around."

"I don't understand. What do you mean *my* earth? You're not from here?" Both Peter and Viktor shook their heads. "You're from another planet?"

"No, actually we're from another realm. It's not unlike this one, but much older than this one is." Peter sat back in his own chair as he explained. "We left Ravengric when Lady Olivia died. It was…she was Viktor's mate. And, yes, the name of the realm is named from my master. He and his family are rulers there. When I was made, my master was approached by his oldest brother, King Dakamon, to come here and see how accepting people would be of our kind. Also, we think now it was…it was to get us away. We never guessed that there would be some of us here, though not as powerful as we are."

"So they didn't come." Peter looked at Viktor, and Brock knew. "They did come to this realm and live here now. Your people, people from your realm."

"Yes. We are thriving here as well as other peoples from other realms. We have had to make some changes in our lifestyle as well as our eating habits. On our realm the ones we feed from are welcoming and ready to give us what we need. We pay them for their services and…." Viktor smiled. "I'm sorry. I digress. I would pay you and your mate well to help us. You wouldn't even need to quit working for your family, but provide us with support when the need arises."

"So we'd be your hit men." Viktor laughed, and Brock smiled. "Not a term you're using, I guess, but it's the same thing."

"Yes, I suppose it is. My kind has heard of the tiger you have within you, but has never seen it. We've heard tales of your strength and power, and know that you cannot be beaten by anything once you've set your mind to finding a rogue. Not by a vampire or any other being because of what it means. There are three to their one, and a strength that can never lose with those odds.

Additionally, there is the fact that you have a matched mate. Someone who would have your back no matter what happens and love you so much that none could come between you. An invincible pair."

"And when we're...we will have children. What happens to them when we're out saving your asses?" Peter started to say something, but Viktor cut him off.

"He's right to say he would be saving our collective asses. And to ease your mind, we would send others to protect them as if they were their own. You can trust me when I say that your children will be as safe as they would if you were with them."

"Sorry, but I don't trust you any more than you do me." Peter stood up, but Brock watched Viktor. When he nodded, Brock leaned back in his chair as Peter sat down.

"You're a very astute man. I like that about you." Brock didn't move, waiting for the proverbial other shoe to drop. When it didn't right away, he decided to push buttons.

"So are you. But this beating around the bush crap is getting us nowhere fast. I have a mate upstairs that is exhausted from taking care of something that, frankly, you two should have taken care of years ago. She's been injured by one of your own, as well as had to endure all kinds of hardships that neither the two of you could even guess. What the fuck do you want?" Brock stood up. "Either say it or get out of my house. I have more important things to do with my time."

Peter was pissed instantly. Brock would have had to have been really stupid not to see it. But when the man stood up and reached for him, his beast reached out as well. Peter snatched his hand back so quickly it might have been comical if the growl falling from his lips hadn't have scared him a little, too. Peter was pulled back and shoved in his chair so quickly that Brock blinked several times to make sure that he'd even moved.

"As I said before, you're a very astute man." Viktor leaned back in his chair again and looked at him. Brock watched him as well. "I want you to work for us more than ever now. You're a man who can get results and someone that I believe is incorruptible as well. A man of great honor."

"Meaning?" Brock knew what the word meant; he just wasn't sure how that applied to him. He wasn't fooled when Viktor smiled either.

"Meaning that having a man like you working for me means that even though I pay your salary, you would have no problem making me toe the line as well. I would expect you would bring me before the council just as quickly as you might anyone. As would your mate, I expect." Viktor pulled an envelope from his pocket and handed it out to him. Brock didn't touch it.

"You want us to work for you doing what? And I mean exactly what would we be doing for you? I don't want any illusions that we'd be paving your driveway with gold or the blood of those who shit in your oatmeal."

"You'd be doing just what you did today. Go after and rid the world of the kind of vermin that the Coles were. There would be a contract on each person or persons you are to take care of, a list of where to find them, and all expenses paid to you of any and all out-of-pocket money you have to use to get the job done. And that would include any downtime you needed afterwards, so long as you don't abuse the perk." He laid the envelope on the desk and stood up. "You should also know that being a hunter like this, you'd have the...let's just call them 'enhanced abilities,' that you do now, plus a few extra that would help you along the way. You call me when you and your mate have made a decision. Either way, you're going to be paid and paid well for what you did for us today."

"You say 'us.' Who are the others?" Viktor smiled and glanced at Peter, who nodded. There was something going on here that he wasn't sure about, but he wasn't going to say anything just yet. He needed to speak to Em, and until then he wasn't saying a word.

"The council that the two of you would be working for is a group of all beings, shifters of every species, as well as every realm. We're called simply the Holders of the Realm."

Brock watched them leave the room. Holders of the Realm he knew about, as did most shifters and anything else that could become something other than their human side. He was still sitting there holding the sealed envelope in his hand when he felt Em wake. He went up the stairs three at a time and watched her stretch. She looked at him and smiled.

"Are you feeling better?" She nodded. "Good. I've missed you. And I need to talk to you about something."

"And on that note, I'm leaving." He looked over at Bronwyn, who he'd completely forgotten about. "You two should turn off your cell phones, lock up the house, and have wild monkey sex in every part of your house. Oh, and you need to buy more furniture. I have a feeling you're going to be entertaining more now."

Brock nodded, not having a clue what she was talking about. He stood in the doorway until he heard the door close in the kitchen and knew that she was gone. He looked at Em.

"I want you." She nodded. "I mean right now and anyway you want. I'll even let you take my cock into your mouth if you want."

She nodded again, and when he moved toward her, she held up her hand and he stopped. She was smiling so big that he found it hard not to smile back at her. When she swallowed several times, he thought she was choking until she spoke.

"I love you, Brock Golden." Good Christ, she could speak.

Chapter 14

Alistair looked over every page of the contracts and found nothing that would come back to bite his brother in the ass. And he'd tried very hard to find something. It was the most beneficial contract for the person it was being issued to that he'd ever seen. It gave them everything and asked for only one thing in return...to kill the bad guys and do it quickly and quietly. Alistair picked up his phone to call his brother when he and Em were suddenly in the doorway.

"If you don't sign this, I will." Brock laughed and kissed Em's hand. "They are paying you extremely well and giving you pretty much anything and everything you want. The Realm is providing you with insurance, household help such as nannies and other services, a limo is at your disposal as well as a jet. That alone will save our company more money than you make now from us."

"And the job, is it what I told you he said it was going to be?" Alistair wasn't really happy with his brother and his mate being called hunters as the contract called them, but they were suited to the job better than anyone he knew. Especially after they were given the gifts that were listed in the contract.

"It is. I'm only concerned about what will happen to any children you have after all this is given to you, but according to Peter it will pass on to your children as well. The best part is you can quit at any time and everything you've been given as part of your job is yours to keep." He looked over at Em and decided there was something different about her. "And as you said, if you have children, they will be cared for by a number of trusted guards until such time as you return."

Brock nodded and looked at Em. When he nodded, Em looked at him and smiled. Alistair felt as if she'd touched him with her smile, and it went through his entire body. There was something definitely different about her.

"We have something to share with you." Alistair just knew his brother was going to tell him they were going to have a baby and waited, excited more than he could say. Just that morning Ally had told him that she was pregnant as well.

"I actually have something to share with you." It took Alistair several seconds before he realized that Em had spoken to him. He stood up and then flopped back down in his chair twice before he found his own tongue.

"You can talk." He flushed when he realized how his voice had squeaked. "Can you hear as well?"

"Yes. It's my gift for helping them with the Coles." Alistair had noticed that she no longer called them her family, and she no longer referred to any of them as her brother or dad. They were just "the Coles."

"I don't know what to say. Congratulations, of course, and you...Christ, love, I'm so happy for you." He looked at his brother, who nodded, and Alistair came around his desk and pulled her into his arms. "I can't think of a more fitting gift to give to you."

Alistair let her go and sat on the edge of the desk as Brock asked him about the contract. He assured him that it was a good bet and recommended that they sign it. Em asked about the enhancements they were going to get once the contract was signed.

"Does it say how we'll get them?" He told her no, but he had a call into Peter and Viktor to have that answered. "I would also like to know if we will have time to get married first before we're assigned any hunting."

"I asked that, and you have three months before they'll call on you. He said that he didn't foresee any problems now, but wanted me to ask you if there was an emergency could you please help them out. He said that you would be given a bonus for helping them if the need arose."

His phone ringing had him going to the other side of his desk to answer it. He asked Viktor if he could put him on speaker phone as both Brock and Em were in his office. The man was happy to say yes, but then said to wait. Seconds later he was standing in his office with another man.

"This is the Holder of the Realm's attorney, Rafael von Drakon. Though he would like to have a word after we have finished here, that has nothing to do with this contract. His is a more personal matter." Alistair nodded, and Viktor looked at Brock and Em. "So you are ready to sign? I have answers to your questions now, too. When you sign the contract, your enhancements will be given to you immediately. And you will have instructions on each of them that will be simple enough to understand."

Brock looked at him, and he nodded and then at Em. She, too, nodded. The contracts were given to Rafael first, who went over it, making sure that he'd made no alterations. Then he showed them where to sign. Then as a witness, Alistair signed as well. Viktor smiled and shook his hand.

"I will leave you now. You have your three months, but as I have requested, if you are needed we would appreciate it if you were to help us out." Both nodded. "Good. Then I leave you."

"Wait. I don't know...." Brock glanced at Em. "We need to know about the extra things. When we'll get them and how to use them, I'm not sure...." Viktor smiled.

"I nearly forgot to give you the instructions." He held out his hand and looked at the two of them. "You understand that with this comes great power. And with this power comes great responsibility. Taking my hand now will give you the knowledge you need to be everything you'll need to do the job."

Brock took his hand first and staggered slightly when he let go. When Em hesitated, Viktor only smiled at her until she took it as well. She was helped gently to the chair by Brock, who still looked a little winded. Alistair asked what happened now.

"Nothing. They are fully ready to help us. I would suggest that you practice your new found powers a little, but you should have no problems." He nodded at them both and disappeared. Brock and Em were still sitting in his office when he took Rafael to an empty office.

"I am impressed with your abilities as an attorney." The man had barely sat when he spoke. "I am in need of an assistant that...oh bother and humbug. What I want is to retire. I have been the Realm's attorney for nearly a thousand years and, frankly, I would like to see the world, this world, again."

"I can help you find yourself someone to either assist you or even to take over when you —" He was shaking his head before Alistair finished. "You don't want my help?"

"Yes and no. I need help, but not with finding anyone. I have found someone to take my place...if he wants to take the job, that is." Alistair was still lost. "You'll help me, won't you?"

"Of course." The man beamed at him and stood up. Alistair took his hand and staggered back a little at the surge of power that danced over him. "What was that?"

"You've made me a very happy man, Alistair. I'll make sure that your contract is sent to you immediately so that you may read it over." Before Alistair could say *oh bother and humbug,* the man was gone. He was still standing in the empty office when Ryland came in.

"Are you all right?" Alistair told him he wasn't sure. "You look like someone hit you with a ball bat in the nuts and you're still trying to decide if you want to fall over or work through it. I usually fall over. I tell myself I'm going to work through it, but it never hap—"

"I think I just got a job working for the Holders of the Realm as their attorney." Alistair sat down and put his head between his legs. "I work for the Holders of the Realm as their attorney."

~~~

Brock was sitting in his home office when Em walked in. He thought her more beautiful every time he saw her. And now that she could speak to him, he couldn't believe his good fortune. She sat in the chair across from him and looked upset. He wanted to ask her what had happened but she hated when he did that, so he waited.

"Were you aware that we can will ourselves from one place to the other?" He knew that but didn't like the way she'd asked. "Apparently, we can transport others, too, if we want."

"Who did you transport, and how pissed are they going to be when we bring him back?" She smiled. "Oh God, I don't like that look."

"It was Roland, but I already brought him back. By the way, we're going to go out to dinner tonight because he is too upset to cook, and I have to go shopping with him tomorrow. Do you think we can afford an update to the kitchen? Like the entire kitchen?" He smiled. "Oh, and we need to redecorate his room. He wants a bigger television and cable, too."

Brock leaned back in his chair. He'd been thinking of the kitchen and it needing a complete overhaul for some time, and he was going to offer Roland the pool house because they never used it for anything other than storage. But this was just too intriguing not to find out what happened.

"Where did you take him?" She looked away. "Emma, where did you take our cook that has him so upset that we're going to go into debt to fix?"

"He said that he would like to have some fresh salmon and some warm baguettes. I needed to practice, so I took him where those things are the freshest." She flushed. "For the record, I had no idea what a baguette was, so France wasn't any place I thought we'd end up, and as for the fresh salmon?"

He was almost afraid to ask. When she turned a brighter shade of red, he asked her where they'd ended up. She mumbled, and he was sure he'd heard her wrong and asked her to repeat it.

"I said we ended up in the middle of Alaska in a wide river. The salmon were fresh, all right. They were jumping all around us as we got wetter and wetter." She looked at him. "Did I tell you that I'm sorry?"

"No, you didn't." He stood up and walked around his desk, trying his best not to laugh. "So you took him to France to buy baguettes, then to Alaska to catch salmon from the middle of a river. And now it's going to cost us an untold amount of money to pay off our wonderful cook and buy him an expensive car too."

"He said he'd forgo the car if we gave him a raise." She flushed again. "I guess I forgot to mention that, too, huh?"

Brock put his hand over his mouth and grinned. This was just too much fun, and he knew that he'd have to give into his humor soon or hurt himself. He lifted her from the chair and held her away from him.

"I'll do anything you like if you don't punish me." Her voice had gone husky, and he felt his cock thicken in his jeans. "I might even be persuaded to let you tie me to the bed if you feel that would be punishment enough."

She knew. When she smiled at him, Brock pulled her to his body and settled her between his legs as he leaned back more. She'd played him, and he loved her for it.

"Did you really take him on that trip?" She told him that she had and he really was mad, but she also knew that he had been planning the remodel anyway and it was a good bargaining chip. "You vixen."

She leaned into his throat and nipped at his shoulder. When she moved her mouth up and over his neck to his ear, he moaned. Her hot breath was making his skin heat all over. He looked up when the door closed and the lock turned.

"I've been practicing that one for an hour. I think it'll come in very handy when the...urge...hits us to have sex somewhere we shouldn't." He cupped her ass and brought her closer to him. "Not to mention if we're being chased by the bad guys."

"I doubt we'll have time to have sex when we're being chased by the bad guys, but it's a nice trick." She moaned when he rocked her over him. "Of course, we might use it more on our honeymoon when we're about to go out and the maid comes to our door. We can simply lock her out."

"I love the way you think." She nipped her way down his throat to the top button on his shirt and opened it. "But that's not all I've been practicing at. What if I told you I could have us in our bed naked before you could say yes?"

He opened his mouth to tell her to do it when he felt the bed beneath him, sheets silky and cool pressed against his hot back and her body warm and soft over his. Rolling her to her back, Brock moved down her body, kissing her, loving her with his mouth. When he reached her hips, he slipped his hands beneath her and lifted her to his mouth and tasted paradise once again.

Her hissed yes had him suckling hard at her clit as his fingers entered her. When she rocked up to his mouth, he rewarded her with deeper thrusts, curling his fingers inside of her and touching her sweet spot. Every time she shuddered, he took more because she was giving him more. Each time he brought her closer, he wanted more, all of her. Finally, when she started to beg him, he opened her nether lips and pressed his thumb over her clit while he drank her nectar, gorged himself on her juices, and became drunk on her scent. Her climax poured over him, her screams, the first he'd heard since she'd been given her gift, were like music to his ears. Brock loved every part of this woman.

When she was lying limply on the bed, he kissed her navel, then her breast. Moving his body up hers, he skimmed over her, touching her with the barest touches as he feathered kisses over every part of her. When he touched her mouth with his, he didn't take but gave her all his love, showed her how much he cherished and needed her.

Even as he slipped inside of her, he felt her tighten around him, pulling him deeper until there was only one of them. Moving into her, Brock told her he loved her, kissed her throat, her mouth, and her eyelids. As he filled her over and over, he showed her with his body how much he worshiped her, needed her. When she pulled him back to her mouth and held him to her, he came. His release felt as if he'd given her his soul as well as his heart. And when he felt her tighten around him again, she wrapped her arms around him and held him to her, and Brock never wanted her to let him go.

Rolling to his back again, he held her as her tremors subsided, her body no longer jerked, and her heart slowed. Even when she slept, he held her, knowing that for as long as he lived, forever and beyond, he would love this woman more and more every day and feel it wasn't enough. Brock Golden was in love with his mate.

Perhaps an hour later she stirred and then lifted her head to look at him. When she smiled at him, he smiled back. She looked so delicious that he wanted her again, but knew that they were going to be late if he had her.

"We're getting married today." He nodded. "Do you really want to? I mean, we can just stay like this for the rest of our lives, and I'll be just as happy."

He kissed her nose. "I'm okay with that. Do you think we can have Roland bring our meals up here? I'm sure it will be awkward for him, but if this is where you want to stay, then I'm okay with that, too."

She slapped his chest. "That's not what I meant, and you know it. I meant we can just live together. Marriage doesn't have to happen for me to be as happy as I am right now."

"You have to tell Mom then." She looked at him wide-eyed, then shook her head. "What? Are you afraid of her too?"

"Damn straight." She got up and went to the bathroom and turned on the water. "I don't know anyone in their right mind who wouldn't be afraid of her. She looks like she's going to be this sweet tiny little lady, then she gets a burr up her butt and you can't seem to get away fast enough."

Brock laughed as he watched her run around the room looking for clothes. When she turned to him, he didn't even try to hide the fact that he was enjoying himself. She looked at his cock, and he wrapped his hand around himself and moaned.

"Come here, Em." She shook her head. "I'm going to have you again, and if you make us late, I'm going to tell my mom that it was entirely your fault, that you flaunted yourself all over the bedroom and I had no choice but to claim you again."

"You would, wouldn't you?" He nodded and rolled his hand up and down his cock. "Can you come that way?"

"Yes." He moved up and down a little faster and a pearl of his cum pebbled at the tip of his cock. "Come here and ride me."

"I'd rather suck you." His cock jerked hard in his hand, and he moaned. "I want to wrap my mouth around you and lick you until you come down my throat. I want to feel your balls fill just before they release."

When she got close enough to the bed to touch her, he pulled her over him and rolled her around. Now her pussy was over his chest. He waited until she leaned over and took him into his mouth before he lifted her up and pulled her over his mouth so that he could eat her. When she bit into his cock, he nearly came up off the bed.

"Gently, love." She moaned when he cupped her ass and brought her tighter against his tongue. Her cream poured from her and right into his mouth. This time he didn't take his time but brought her to a swift climax even as his balls tightened against his body.

"Come for me, Brock. Give me your cum." When she took his balls in her warm hands and rolled them, he broke through the tight muscles of her ass and bit her clit. She screamed. And he roared.

His cock jettisoned into her waiting mouth like he had in her sheath. Even as he brought her to another climax, then another, she cried out for more. Rolling her to her back, he sat up on the bed. When she moved to her belly, he lifted her ass up and plunged deep into her pussy. Riding her as hard as he could, he leaned down and whispered in her ear.

"Come. Come now and I'll mark you." She took his hand and guided him to her pussy. When he pinched her clit, she came apart and he sank his teeth deep into her shoulder. His own climax raced toward the peak and leapt over until he was sure he'd never survive the fall. Sealing the deep wound, he threw back his head and roared out, letting anyone who was within hearing know that he'd claimed his mate.

There was going to be no hope for it. They were going to be late, and he didn't care. When she went limp beneath him, he rolled them to their backs and let himself slip away with her. Christ, his mom was going to be pissed.

Chapter 15

"Ryland Golden, this is not the least bit funny and you know it." He nodded, afraid to speak or lose the barely held control over his laughter. "You know as well as I do what they're doing, and I'm not the least bit happy about it. They were supposed to be here twenty minutes ago."

Ryland had just contacted his brother, and they were on their way. He couldn't even tell his mom that because there was just no way he was going to open his mouth. Not yet at any rate. When she glared at him, he lifted his daughter to his face and hid his laughter in her cherub cheeks.

"If you think I don't know what you're doing, you're wrong, young man. Laughing at your own mom is not going to get you brownie points when you'll need those most. I'm ready to kick all your bottoms right now." She turned when he stood up. Brock and Em were just suddenly there.

"Hi, Mom. I'm sorry we're late, but it's all Em's fault." Brock laughed when Em slugged him. "But we do have an announcement to make. It's been hard to keep quiet, but well… I'll let Em explain."

They all looked at her, and she flushed. When she lifted her hands up, Ryland wanted to tell her that she needed to go slow for him, that learning sign language wasn't as easy as he'd thought it would be. In fact, it was damned hard. She smiled at them.

"I can talk now." No one moved, and he felt his own mind sort of seize up. "It was one of the many gifts I received for our help in taking care of the Coles."

Ryland looked at his family, then back at her. She was embarrassed, he could tell. When she moved to stand behind Brock, he looked at his brother. He wasn't happy with them either. Ryland moved to stand in front of her and handed his daughter to Brock.

"I don't think I've ever known anyone to render this family speechless before." He lifted her chin when she bowed her head. "Oh no you don't, look at me."

She lifted her head up, and he could see the tears in her eyes. They had hurt her by not being happy. Ryland didn't even ask for permission from Brock, but picked up Em and swung her around the room several times until she laughed. He put her down and looked at the rest of them with a raised brow. His mom was the first to react.

"I'm...good heavens child, you've a beautiful voice and to...I just don't know how to tell you how happy I am." She, too, pulled her into her arms and sobbed a little. "You must be so happy. I am too. I'm...darling, say something to me."

"I was afraid you thought I was a freak." His mom looked upset. "You don't really seem all that happy."

"Well, frankly, I'm not. And it has nothing to do with your speaking. And now that I think on it, you should have called me. You have a voice, use it." Ryland started to pull Em into his arms again when his mom winked at Em. "You're going to have to tell me how this came to pass. I'm excited to hear. But I want you as my daughter right now. Come along. Let's get this show on the road, shall we?"

Ryland looked at Brock as Em was being towed away. "What the hell just happened? Did she just reprimand your mate for not calling her to tell us you were going to be late?"

"I think she did. Yes, I do believe my mom just yelled at my mate...who could hear her and speak right back at her too." Brock smiled. "And you wouldn't believe the other little gifts we got to play with now that we're going to be working for the Realm. Christ, we can teleport to anywhere."

Brock told him the story about Roland and the fish while they waited on the judge. He was still laughing when his brother Keith came in. He was just telling him the story when Bronwyn touched his mind.

"So? Is this a bachelor party or a wedding?" Laughing, he told her both. *"Not funny, big boy. Your mom is waiting on the six of you to come out, and she's taking your lateness out on me. I'm ready to turn her into something."*

"I wouldn't if I were you. I'm not sure if she can actually do it, but she might just get you back. She's very resourceful when she wants to get you." Bronwyn agreed. *"Besides, we're ready when you are."* Ryland told her they were coming out now.

Em had begged for the courthouse wedding. She had no family, save her mom, and she wasn't able to leave the hospital just yet. Peter had told him she more than likely never would be able to either. Her mind had snapped, and she seemed to like where she was, in a place where there were no vampires or anything else that went bump in the night.

Em was supposed to go and visit her twice now but had canceled both times. Ryland didn't blame her. When Peter had said he'd looked in on her, Em had asked to speak to him privately. After they came out of the office a good hour later, Em had gone out into the yard and shifted. Bronwyn had told him not to follow. She had to fight her own demons.

It had been over two hours before she'd come back into the house, and he knew that she had been talking to Brock. When she came in, he took her into his arms and held her. Soon after he and his mom had left them. He was very proud of his newest family member.

An hour later, Brock was kissing his bride. When he'd slipped the large diamond on Em's finger, she had looked up at him, shocked, but said nothing. Her hands were trembling when she put Brock's ring on his finger. When the judge started to pronounce them man and wife, Em stopped him. She said she had something to say.

"I wanted to say that I'm not just marrying Brock and taking him as my husband, but I'm taking you all as my family. I don't expect for you to want me to call you *Mom*," she told his mom, "but in my heart you will be. All of you are not my in-laws, but my brothers and sisters, more than I'd ever had before. Children of yours will be as my own, and I will protect them with all that I am. I have not just fallen in love with Brock, but with all of you."

His mom sniffled and then put her hands on her hip. "Well the sooner you let him say the best part—you know, the pronouncement?—we can claim you as well. Get on with it, girl. Oh, and if you call me *Mom*, I will be honored."

Bronwyn kissed her cheek and whispered to her. His mom blushed slightly and hugged her. He wasn't sure, but he thought his mom was going to be *Mom* to all of them by the end of the day. Ryland nodded his head at his mate when she winked at him. Christ, he loved her so much.

The reception was being held at their house. Bronwyn didn't cook, but she could order a catering service around like a drill sergeant. By the time Brock and Em were ready to cut the cake, they'd been served steak and baked potatoes and warm rolls. Not a vegetable in sight either.

Ryland looked at his two remaining single brothers. Keith didn't look like he cared if he ever got a mate. He was having too much fun flirting with any female he could find, and it mattered little to him if they were nine or ninety. He simply loved women.

But his brother Jules looked at Em and Brock with longing, much the same as he had with Neal and Alistair when they were mated. He wanted someone in his life…someone that would be with him and go to his shows and be supportive. He wanted someone to talk to, read with, and simply be with. Ryland had a feeling his mate was going to be just the opposite of what he wanted.

She would be hard, opinionated, as well as sarcastic and…he looked at his own mate and smiled. A great deal like the rest of the women in this streak. Ryland was pretty sure that was why Jules dated the quiet and reserved type. He just didn't think he could handle the type of women they all had.

"He'll be fine." He looked at his mom. "Jules, he'll be fine. His mate is out there, and when she finds him or him her, they will be perfectly matched just like the rest of you are."

"I don't think so." She looked at him. "I think his mate is going to be like the rest of the women here, but more. I think she's going to give him a run for his money. And I, for one, can't wait to meet her."

"You're wishing for him to have a hard time of it?" He shook his head. "Then what? Surely you can't want him to suffer? He's a very quiet boy, and his mate will be just what he needs."

"Oh, I'm sure she will be. And as for suffering? We all suffered. But look what we got in return; mates that bring out the best in all of us."

~~~

Peter didn't want to tell them that there were more out there. He didn't want to disturb their day. But they'd had word just that morning that two more of Jimmy's children were out and making the human world a scary place. Instead of telling them, he let the young couple leave the house and be driven to the airport.

"They will need to return soon." Peter nodded at Viktor. "You are a good man to let them have this. I would have been too harsh with them and made them stay, I believe."

Peter didn't believe that for a minute, but said nothing. The man had as soft a heart as he did when it came to love. He did want the best for the Goldens and their mates. He had come to love them as his own.

"Do you really believe they can help us, or do you think they will only help us to a point?" Peter looked at Viktor when he didn't answer him. "You are not sure, are you? You do not know what will happen to them or their family."

"They will be safe, this I'm sure of. Will they help us? I'm positive of that more than I am anything. The only problem I foresee is that they will not quit until they have vanquished all the evil in the world and harm only themselves. Exhaustion can be just as harmful as a bullet, as you are well aware."

Peter did. When the Coles had started out, he'd worked during the day and watched them at night as they came closer to his friends. He wanted to kill them, but knew that he could not. Even Viktor had had to live by the rules that he'd set forth when they'd arrived.

"When will you tell them?" Peter thought about it and didn't have a clue. The rogues had done nothing more than kill a single person, which was bad enough, but they had lain low since then.

"It will be soon. But not until they need to know." He sighed. "When we came to this world, master, did you ever think there would be such destruction by the very people that we wanted to learn from? Did you think that they would kill one another as if they were nothing more than bugs under their shoes?"

"Nay, I did not. I believed that this was going to be the start for our overpopulated world; a place to come and have a rest from our own world when we needed it. I never thought that we'd have to work hard so that the humans wouldn't be killed by the very hands that we thought to be friends with." Peter nodded. "I have spoken to my brother and told him of the couple we have found. He would like to meet them."

Peter stood up straighter when he thought of the king. He'd loved the man before he'd come here, and now...now he knew him for what he was. He looked at his master and wondered what he knew of his brother. Probably a good deal more than Peter did.

"I believe that they would be honored to meet him, but once they learn what we have done, there will be hell to pay, I think. The Goldens would put out the Ritz, as I have heard them say." Peter wasn't sure what that meant really, but he knew that it was akin to putting out the best for someone. And maybe their best would not be what they might think of at first. The king was a tyrant and an evil man. "Mrs. Bronwyn would make him jealous of her ability to make things happen. Hopefully he will wait until the other two arrive."

She actually scared them both. Not that either of them thought she'd harm them, but she was indeed the strongest cat they knew, with the exception of her mate. And when she was angry, which he'd seen her be, then she was very vengeful. Especially when she was protecting what she felt was hers.

"I will make sure of it. They will all need to be together before he comes here. If not...if not, then all will be lost. But I do believe you're right. He may demand she go back with him. I do not believe she'd go, but I'm willing to bet she'd give him a few pointers to get him on the right path." Peter nodded. Of that he had no doubt.

"I will be leaving soon. I have to work in the morning at the shop, and then I will make sure that the children of Jimmy's are laying low. I would ask that I could put them into a deep sleep until the couple has had their honeymoon." Viktor nodded. "I shall see you on the morrow then?"

"No. I must return to my own castle this night. When my brother comes, and I believe it will be soon, I should like to have the place aired and cleaned for him and his entourage. If he decides to bring one, which I've no doubt that he will." Peter embraced his maker. "You will be well then?"

"I will. I have made the arrangements for the tigers. Their accounts have been set up, and their payments have been set aside. They didn't ask you for their payment amount, did they?" Viktor said they hadn't. "I know a little about money here, and what they are to receive will be considered a wealth for one year. We will pay them that for a lifetime, but I'm sure that it will not be enough considering what they will be doing for us. But I believe they will be pleased."

"Or mad." They both nodded. "I should like to know what they say when they find out. It will make me laugh, I'm sure, on more than one occasion. I would imagine that they would have a great deal to say to you when they find out."

Peter thought about letting them find out on their own and making himself unavailable for a few weeks. Or maybe a few years. He smiled when he knew that wasn't going to work either. He might as well simply tell them and told his master he would take care of it straight away.

After Viktor left, Peter sat in his room with his plants. His trees were doing so well that he knew that he'd have to transplant them into bigger pots soon. And his seedlings were now big enough to be put into the bigger pots he'd already prepared for them. He lifted the small violet and blew across the soft leaves and watched them shiver. These were his favorite of all he owned, and he had nearly every color that the young Rayne had in her shop.

"When I next go to visit my master, I will take you to him as a gift. He always fusses at me for bringing him plants, but I have seen his room where he keeps them, and he takes pride in them. His room is becoming as grand as mine, I think." Peter looked around. "Perhaps it's time I expanded your room and brought in more light for you. Would you like that, my little ones?"

They didn't speak to him as they did to Rayne, but he knew that they would love him for it. He thought about the yard beyond this room and decided that he would make the calls to make the room larger in the morning. Perhaps one of the Goldens could recommend a good firm that could do the work for him. Peter would see Neal in the morning and ask him for help.

Going to his bedroom, he looked at the sky light that he'd had installed a few weeks ago. He'd never dreamed that he'd ever have the opportunity to have the sun warm his face in the mornings and watch, when the mood suited him, the sun set in the late evening. His life had taken a great change in the past few months.

Reaching out to the children, he put them to sleep, knowing that once they woke, their hunger would be great. He was sorry for it but knew that he had to give the couple a few days to rest so that when they found the rogues, they would be strong enough to battle them without getting hurt themselves. He loved them too much to even want them scratched.

Soon, he thought, soon he'd be able to help bring them to justice. Smiling, Peter thought of the rogues and how they would react when tigers showed up to bring them to an end. Closing his eyes, Peter touched the others in the streak to make sure they were safe.

When he was assured they were, he also reached to the others — the mates of the two remaining Golden children — and made them safe as well. When he realized that both women were up and about, doing what they did best, he left them to it, knowing that they would fight him and wear themselves out more if he tried to get them to rest for the days to come. Jules was not going to be happy with him, he thought.

Peter finally let sleep take him.

About the Author

Kathi Barton, author of the bestselling series Force of Nature, lives in Nashport, Ohio with her husband Paul. In addition to writing full time Kathi likes to spend time with her eight grandkids, three children and three children-in-laws. She writes to relax and have fun.

Her muse, a cross between Jimmy Stewart and Hugh Jackman brings them to life for her readers in a way that has them coming back time and again for more. Her favorite genre is paranormal romance with a great deal of spice. You can visit Kathi on line and drop her an email if you'd like. She loves hearing from her fans. aaronskiss@gmail.com.

Follow Kathi on her blog:
http://kathisbartonauthor.blogspot.com/

www.ingramcontent.com/pod-product-compliance
Lightning Source LLC
Chambersburg PA
CBHW032128170626
46808CB00006B/2148